BREECH BABY

Being born upside down should give you a leg up.

ED. RYAN

THE
NEW
VAGUE

Published by The New Vague
244 5th Avenue
Suite E287
New York, New York
10001

ISBN 978-0-9912348-9-9

Printed in the United States of America

Cover design by Ed Ryan

For my loved ones, and yours, without whom nothing is possible...or worthwhile.

PART I

ONE

"HELLO THERE, CUTIE. What's your name?" she said, as she balanced a pair bifocals on the end of her long, twisted nose.

Such odd angles for a nose, I thought, like half-cooked spaghetti. This twisted proboscis made her look like she hailed from Salem, her family tree featured prominently in the encyclopedia of Wicca. But it was just the opposite. She was quite sweet, and young. Too young for glasses anyway, but whatever it took to see me in all my glory.

I barreled over the wannabe Benjis, Cujos, and Lassies, desperate to reach the front of the cage. Puppies in cages. Can you imagine? What will they cage next, birds?

They love to domesticate, to tame, to strip, to distill the real life out of life. It makes them feel safe, I suppose, because it calms the savage beast, and decreases competition.

When I was a lion on the Serengeti, we had our own method of pruning the competition. We shared the plain with the cheetah, a fellow member of the feline family but a threat nonetheless, or so we felt. A grown cheetah was the fastest cat in the wild and we couldn't collar it. The baby, however, was easy prey. The female hides her cubs in the brush when she goes hunting. That's when we lions came to pay our respects. It was terribly gruesome, but I couldn't object. Had I acted any differently I'd seem like an out-of-the-ordinary lion, and they'd have ripped me to pieces also. The carnage was quick and strangely merciful, but in the end it was a massacre, loud, bloody, and violent. Much like birth itself.

Domestication is far more creative. I'll give people credit for that. That and Q-Tips.

What was I just saying?

She stuck her finger through the bars and I mashed my face against it, getting my fill of feel. If there's one thing I miss, my feral friend, it is being touched. The activation of an entire system from the stimulation of a single nerve ending is an undersung phenomenon.

I looked up and smiled. She returned the gesture and again, angles. Angles and metal. But even through the dental dementia her warmth shone. I already felt like I was at home lying on a shag rug in

< 2 >

front of an electric heatilator, UL-approved.

I had seen her type before. They paraded through the shelter daily, looking for a rescue, something to keep them from climbing the nearest water tower and relinquishing a short life of humble hopes. A suicide note was pointless. Why explain the obvious? They needed something very simple: puppy love.

"Can I help you folks?" Arby inquired.

Arby was the caretaker and purveyor of us unwanteds. To the shallow eye he was simply a cleaner of cages, a brusher of coats, and a lecturer on the newest developments in flea control. But Arby did more than that. Much more. He doled out companionship, real live love in the fur.

He had a great vibe, a lulling low frequency. Sure, he oscillated, like everyone, but never more than a few semitones, and then only in the most stressful of circumstances, like when he had to retrieve a retriever from unfit parents. That can be a dangerous undertaking, tearing loved ones apart. People get attached to things, all sorts of things for all sorts of reasons, logical and ill. I knew a guy attached to a telephone because that's where he thought his friends were. It seems to me you should keep your friends in your heart and in your mind, because if you lose your phone you'll be awfully lonely. But if you lose your mind, you'll still have company.

At the shelter, Arby and his team screened all prospective parents. There were questionnaires, credit

< 3 >

checks, and interviews. He searched and researched, and followed up with surprise visits. He needed to be sure his children were being properly taken care of. He was a good man. I would have called him "friend," but we didn't speak the same language.

"Yes," she replied to Arby. "My name is Sous. This is my husband." Warden, I think she said. I don't have much to say about him. Not that he defies description. He just doesn't deserve any.

My tail was wagging when we arrived at their home. It was a modest ranch with plenty to be grateful for. Bryan even wrote a poem about it. Bryan. I'm getting to him.

Sous took good care of me. She held me, petted me, read me bedtime stories and, once or twice upon a midnight dreary, she crooned a "Frere Jacques" as she lay me down to sleep. That might sound weird, singing to a puppy, but I found her voice pacifying.

The poem? The poem went:

The shades were wide open. The kitchen was clean.
Fancy, a room for a washing machine.
With more space to offer. Two bedrooms. A spare?
Someday, if I grow up, I can sleep there?
Picture this picture, the lawn manicured.
And into this picture pure world we were lured.
Handing me over. "He's yours." Smiles spread.
And sugarplum fairies danced 'round in my head,
As they sugarplum coated the clues of the dread.

< 4 >

I remember Arby's last visit. He was all smiles, satisfied his work here was done. As he disappeared in his Focus, any and all pretense of domestic bliss went with him.

It didn't take long to see why her nose was crooked.

Warden ruled the roost from a La-Z-Boy recliner. Seldom did he interact with me or Sous. Most of his time was spent with his ears on a television set and his eyes on a tabloid newspaper. I think he spoke so infrequently because it took him that long to develop a thought. That he could breathe was surprising, and unfortunate. I hated him. And those are strong words coming from a puppy.

Unwilling to share his wife's attention, he became incensed when she saw to my needs. His uncontrollable temper leapt from simmer to boil in a flash.

In the interest of self-preservation, Sous began to neglect me. There was no more training, playing, reading, or singing. Not that I needed to go to doggy day school, but an occasional toss of a ball or tug-of-war would've been appreciated. Anything to keep the wheels turning. They say an idle mind is the devil's canvass, if you believe in Beelzebub.

When Warden blew a fuse, Sous would hide me in a sideboard for safekeeping. It wasn't a fancy piece of furniture, just some cheap pressed wood with a laminate finish, but it was better than a refrigerator. If he wanted to batter me he'd have to find me,

<5>

and that required more effort than the mean mister could muster. He was only motivated enough to break what was within reach, so if I disappeared early, I could go the day un-bruised.

I still heard the onslaught, though. It was extremely disconcerting, like brunch with the cheetahs. I tried to tune them out by occupying myself with the contents of my engineered enclosure. It was a treasure chest of textbooks, magazines, catalogues, and travel brochures.

Although I didn't understand the scribble, I loved the pictures. I wondered what made these subjects so worthy of immortalization? Why would someone make them keepsakes?

But wondering is tantamount to chasing your tail, which after a while is dizzying. The answers lay in the captions, so I did what any industrious puppy would; I taught myself how to read. I figured with all that time on my hands I should develop my brain, I mean, if I wasn't going to be fetching. Decoding the symbols was fairly easy. The really hard part was turning the pages. Any dog'll tell you, that is rough.

Once I learned how to learn, Warden and Sous became irrelevant. I had no need of them other than to receive sustenance, and even that was becoming rarer than steak tartare. Home-cooked meals turned to table scraps, then to some paste that tasted like dog food.

Oftentimes I found myself alone in the living

<6>

room, my empty belly rumbling as I stared up at the stucco ceiling, wondering what it would taste like. A lightly-browned meringue with a hint of lime. No surprise, as stucco is made with hydrated lime. Good stucco, anyway.

Now I admit, I've always been prone to flights of fancy. I enjoy a good daydream as well as, maybe more than, a wakened moment. But when it comes to food, every now and then you need a serving of reality.

One silent night, not a creature was stirring. Warden and Sous had retired without putting anything in my bowl. I needed food, and only they could provide it. Waking Warden would ignite fireworks, but malnutrition is risky also. It's the predecessor to many defects. So I let it rip.

"I! Wahh! Am! Wahh! Hungry!"

Light flooded the hallway as the bedroom door opened. The clod clopped through the house like a drunken rhinoceros. I knew from his first step he was not coming to feed me.

I'd been hit by a poacher's Jeep when I was a lion, a tennis racket when I was a bat, and antibiotics when I was a bacterium. It takes its toll. You never quite function the same afterwards.

He hit me only a few times, but they were quality blows. I remember his hands were soft from being so unused.

"You done cryin'?" he growled.

< 7 >

He could have left it there. Instead, he picked me up. Sous shrieked at the top of her lungs, a distressing farewell, before I was launched on my maiden voyage. I'm surprised he didn't break a bottle of champagne over my head, as is customary on such occasions.

I thought being a puppy would be easy. I'd be cute and cuddly and in return be loved and adored. Such a simple mission.

The brick mantel quickly approached. This was going to mean damage, bruises and broken bones. Pain, my ephemeral friend, is a feeling I don't miss.

So I left.

<8>

TWO

YOU'D THINK A million years of evolution would develop a shell so impenetrable that not nobody not no how could get at you. Yet there I was, running for my life, as only a turtle can.

Call me cowardly, but my entire family had been slaughtered before my very eyes, devoured by the dive-bombing boobies and frigate birds that patrolled the airspace above the Galapagos Islands. The beach was littered with empty shells, the skies ablaze with beaks and wings. It must have been like Normandy on D-Day, only those brave souls were running toward the land. I was running in the opposite direction, toward the water. So I guess in my case it was more like ab-Normandy.

I was struck hard and rolled onto my back. That's how they prepare you for extraction. They turn you over, expose your soft underbelly, and rip you from your shell. I flailed my arms and legs wildly, hoping to roll back onto my front. But once a turtle has turned, its odds of recovery are between zero and zilch. It's how they were designed, the natural order of things, and when you mess with the natural order of things, things get messy.

All I could do was withdraw into my shell until some semblance of normalcy was restored.

I haven't the foggiest idea of how long I was hidden before the cavalry arrived. Over the hill they strode, heavily armed with plastic bottles, cameras, and sunscreen. Tourists! In all my lives, I was never so happy to see people.

The skies cleared as my winged predators withdrew, frightened off by the platoon of their undeclared yet natural-born enemies.

As always, the group had a leader, a tour guide. He advised the rubberneckers to stay back as he walked out onto the protected sand, picked me up, and posed for photographs. The gentle giant fielded questions about my evolution, habitat, and heritage. He even knew who my mother was. I never knew her. She dropped me off ages ago and never returned. But I didn't mind. Turtles don't care about that sort of thing. They're far too evolved.

Still, it would've been nice to have someone special. She didn't have to nurse me or anything, just help me out of a jam on occasion, like today.

<10>

After the last snapshot, the tour guide carefully placed me back on the beach, and the sand simians departed for the next scenic overlook.

I recommenced my journey to the safe and sound. Once in the ocean, I'd never have to leave, only pop my head up occasionally for air. I was so close I could taste it.

Then, all went black.

I was sure I'd been gored by the beak of some wanting fowl, that some friggin' frigate bird had returned to finish me off. And my ending began.

I drifted out of time and mind, to a place deeper and darker than my own prehistoric shell. I thought dying would hurt, but it was painless. I was without senses. I wasn't being mauled or chewed or regurgitated into the mouths of baby boobies. I wasn't 'Being' anything. I could see nothing, feel nothing, hear nothing. It was as if I had disappeared. But I was still there, somewhere, aware.

Fuzzy, buzzy, and unclear, there were ears and shells and claws and hair, some of me, some of him, twisted and scattered, strung together in the shards of a mirror shattered.

And the eyes. Those eyes. Those black, stupefying eyes.

We were in a bathroom with hard surfaces, tiles, porcelain, and stainless steel. The fluorescent lights buzzed interminably.

"Bryan... Bryan..." she said, she said. The sound

< 11 >

was so reverberant, it echoed.

A woman stood in the doorway. "Did you take that from the beach?" she asked, referring to me.

He looked at her and turned away, looking again in the mirror at the disarray that was us.

"Answer me, young man!"

Again he said nothing, his only acknowledgment the slight crack of a twisted smile. Until that moment I hadn't realized how tense he was, how much pressure he was putting on my shell. He began to relax. His grip loosened. It felt good.

She tried to grab me from his hand. I was dropped on the floor, landing next to a hypodermic needle. It was the same one that had retarded my sprint to the ocean just before I disappeared. Bryan must have accidentally scooped us up together. It was only a syringe, actually. The needle was gone, probably gobbled up by a dolphin who thought it was a needlefish, or a pollock who thought it was a lure. I was glad to see someone cared enough about the ocean to try to inoculate it, but that non-degradable plastic cylinder and fifty feet of virgin sand had been all that stood between me and my destination, so pardon me if I don't wax Hippocratic.

"Do you know how much trouble we'll get in if they see you took something from the beach?" she said, as she picked me up. "That's a very special beach, sweetheart. You can't take souvenirs. If you want a friend, we'll get you one when we get home. But this

< 12 >

one has to stay here. OK?"

She looked him in the eyes. I felt her hand twitch and tighten around me as he looked back at her with his desolate gaze.

A film of nervous perspiration began to coat her palm. She headed toward the bathroom stall and I knew exactly where this was going.

The porcelain graveyard. The traditional unwanted pet cemetery. I'd be sent to the all-consuming, all-accepting sewer, where I'd drift further to confusion, wandering for years like Moses. His parents set him adrift, too, his real parents, not his turtle parents. He's lucky they didn't anchor him with the Ten Commandments before they dropped him in the drink, or he'd have sunk straight to the bottom, taking his slew of sayings with him. And where would we be without such tabloid truisms as: Thou shalt not omit adultery. Thou shalt not convert. Donor, thy father and mother.

Why is it when you heard voices back then, it was scripture? When you hear voices today, it's crazy? Imagine, a thimbleful of Thorazine and religion may never have been invented.

Just because things worked out for this bloke Moses didn't mean I was going to bet the desert on some sewer pipe dream. They weren't going to throw out this baby with the bathwater.

So I left.

<13>

THREE

BRYAN WAS A young boy from a small, some might say obtuse, family. The three of them lived on an estate on the north shore of a very long island. It was named, this island, I kid you not, Long Island. You laugh now, but after a while it grates on your nerves. The estate came equipped with lots of land, an oversized mansion, two pools, and two parents, Earnie and Avarice Foster, I believe their names were. But I could be wrong. They all sounded alike to me.

Though legal tender is not ancestral, it does tend to be passed from generation to generation. This family was no exception. Earnie's grandfather, Grandfather Earnie, plugged into alternating current with a fella named Tesla, the real smart guy in the electrical field. Almost nobody ever heard of Tesla. His name isn't on the marquis of electricity because he wasn't as conniving and cutthroat as Edison, whose bright idea it was to foist the vastly inferior "direct current" upon a hapless society.

Edison would stop at nothing to get his name on a patent. He's the guy who electrocuted Topsy the elephant and filmed it in order to demonstrate the dangers of alternating current. As if direct current wouldn't render the same results. They'll fry an innocent bystander to death just to prove a point, even if that point is untrue. This is what passes for intelligence. It's a miracle anyone survives. But power corrupts, and currency corrupts absolutely.

What was I just saying? Bryan.

It was advantageous I began as a child and not a more mature figure, say, a SETI scientist or some other higher-up. An adult already has a cadre of friends and predictable patterns. Once I gained a foothold, their behavior might change. Peers would notice. They'd question and scrutinize and I'd have to confabulate some elaborate explanation. A youngster, on the other hand, has not yet inaugurated a personality, so nobody would be the wiser. Not that anyone's wisdom ever much factored into my decision-making.

Though he was perfect for me, Bryan was not a perfect specimen. One of his incisors was badly chipped, which gave it a fang-like appearance. He was very thin and his left collarbone protruded so sharply that if he shrugged his shoulders it could

<15>

very well poke out an eye, or an ear. He walked with a slight limp or, as the doctors would say, an awkward gait, which only exaggerated his asymmetric appearance.

Don't misunderstand me. He was no Dracula meets Quasimodo. He didn't don a cape and drag his feet through the muddy midnight streets, drooling from the corner of his mouth, lugging his engrossed shoulder around like an oversized carry-on bag. He was quite handsome, actually, for those who could see him, with a charming, crooked smile, a sharp wit, and a unique sense of humor. He was just slightly askew. It was as if he and his body were separated at birth, then reunited after a few years of quarantine. They needed some time to get reacquainted.

I wasn't sure why my doppelganger was configured so. He bore little resemblance to his parents. They were both short with light features. Avarice had Caribbean blue eyes. Earnie's were a see of green. The differences went beyond genetic. They were verbose and sociable. Bryan was quiet and shy. They were judgmental. Bryan was observant. They contorted to conform. Bryan was an original, one of a kind.

It defied all sense, yet there he stood, a double helix Statue of Liberty, offering the poor, tired, recessive genes of the world a humble vessel where they could randomly combine. And so they did, to form a life more extraordinary than any I had inhabited in my travels along the food chain.

< 16 >

Bryan had an extremely refined sense of hearing. We heard things nobody else could, conversations from other rooms, other places, people completely out of sight, yet they were as clear as my own voice. When we listened to a symphony, we could hear the players turning their sheet music. Even the loveliest Bach trumpet's valves frequently need oiling, and seldom is there a trombone player whose embouchure doesn't hiss slightly on one side.

His hyper-acuity to the audible spectrum combined with my own sensitivity to the inaudible was often a liability, at times impounding us in a beehive of frivolous stimulus. Even in rural areas the airwaves are crowded, and almost all transmissions fell into our combined perceptual range. Picture listening to every electronic device, every radio, telephone, and television, all at once. It boggles the mind.

I managed to filter out enough to avoid a state of total confusion, most of the time, but it required a lot of energy to stay focused. I was hoping to develop an immunity to the inanity, but it only got worse. For every tack I took, they counter-attacked, broadening the spectrum, increasing bandwidth, adding channels, expanding the distribution network, and always, always, increasing the voltage.

When everything else fails, turn it up.

Of the attributes I loved about Bryan, and there were many, it was his eyes that I cherished the most. They were darker than a black hole, with as much

<17>

gravity. He could recite a simple nursery rhyme but accompanied by his arresting gaze, it would wring dry your corpuscles, blow the dust from your brittle bones, and leave you staring blindly into the sunset, shadow-less, your shrunken head hanging on the trophy wall of his occipital lounge. They were mirrors without reflection. Nobody got in. And nothing got out. I knew they would keep me safe. It was there, behind those lifeless eyes, I hid.

Remaining hidden was imperative. It takes only a few seconds of the International Explorer Channel to confirm: should they ever discover me, my rainforest friend, they will destroy me. No matter how hidden or remote, no matter how deep one burrows or high one flies, no matter if you're an ugly duckling or a beauty quean, an oddball or an even Steven, good or evil, left or right. They always come for you. They always find you. They always destroy you. It is their one instinct that is not extinct.

I knew my mission was a matter of life or death and, could I remember it, I was sure the fate of the entire universe rested upon my shoulders, which were now Bryan's. Whatever I did, it would be with him. He was more qualified than anyone to help me find a reason, a clue, or best of all, you. And the estate was a perfect headquarters from which to work. We planned to stay there a long time.

The parents and the district had other plans.

< 18 >

FOUR

AVARICE WAS NERVOUS. The tap tap click clack of her fake nails on the kitchen countertop wrought havoc on Bryan's eardrums. It was an acute pain, like a needle or an ice pick. And worse, it scrambled her innate transmissions, so I couldn't get a clear read on her frame of mind.

She was an OctaVarian. Her vibe swept over entire octaves in the blink of an eye. Very unstable. She'd been on edge for a while. Apparently being a parent was not what she'd signed up for. I'd been there less than a year and she'd already had occasion to solicit expert opinions of Bryan's eccentricities. Little did she know, it was only going to get worse. Or maybe she did know, which explained her chipping away at the granite.

I thought maybe her finger-tapping was some

kind of secret code, indecipherable, as unrecognizable as the eggs on Bryan's plate, which she hastily threw together without the help of a cook. She had very little experience with cooking. She had very little experience with anything. When you're reared in a place called Shelter Island, I ask you.

The intercom for the front gate sounded. Avarice exhaled audibly and buzzed them in. Normally she would have picked up the handset to see who was there. Something was definitely amiss.

Bryan slowed his intake while I assessed the situation.

Avarice patted down her hair, pulled the creases out of her blouse, and cleared her throat. Cautiously, she turned to Bryan and in a crackly voice forced out, "OK, sweetie. It's time for school." She took his hand and led him outside.

"But there's still food on my plate," Bryan said.

"The bus is here," she responded.

"But you usually make me finish everything on my plate."

"Today's different. Today's your first day of school."

Out we went into the late summer air. It was heavy, humid air, difficult to pass through, clinging to the skin like spider webs. The little yellow bus stood out starkly against the foliage. I loved foliage, but I never learned to appreciate the juxtaposition of leaves and pine needles. Some things go together,

<20>

and some don't.

We approached with extreme caution. The bus was pulsating, struggling to muzzle an energy we had never witnessed. It was like an overstuffed, over-heated popcorn machine, its kernels exploding in full kinetic frenzy.

Children! A baker's dozen.

If anyone could see me, it was they. And just be-cause we were all children and should have a bond, as do you and I, these little people would turn on me in an instant for something bright and fizzy.

Never assume others are like you. They are not. You may find common ground and believe you are alike, that you have the same energy, a vibe, that your stars are aligned, that you're two of a kind, but when push comes to shove your list of differences will far outweigh your list of similarities.

The door opened, and lights began flashing.

"Get on the bus, sweetie," Avarice said, with a sug-gestive palm pushing firmly on Bryan's back.

"But I don't wanna go," he whimpered.

I threw in the puppy-dog eyes as we tried to tug on her heartstrings, but they were too frayed. I was hop-ing her maternal instinct would engage and she'd take pity on her child, but she had apparently left it on the vanity earlier that morning when she put on her face.

"You have to go to school. Everyone does. It's where you read books and learn about the world."

<21>

"I've already done that."

"Don't be silly," she dismissed, steering him to the bus door. "Please, be a darling."

High up in his command post, the driver smiled down in an unassuming pitch. "Hey there, little guy. Coming aboard?"

"No," Bryan said, as he tried to hold his ground.

"Come on. It's not that bad. Have a seat up here by me."

Avarice threw a candy bar to the bus driver, hitting him in the forehead. "Look! The driver has candy."

"You said never go with strangers who offer you candy."

That's my boy. You see why I liked him? Sharp as a razor, and quick on his feet.

Avarice placed both hands in the center of his back, adding leverage as her coaxes went from co-quettish to committed. Bryan dug in his heels, admirably holding his own. Finally, Avarice grabbed him by the collar and shoved.

"No!" Bryan yelled, as he spread his limbs, clinging to the sides of the door. "NO!"

You'd think a rational person would have withdrawn her attack, regrouped, and devised an alternate plan, and you'd be right. But Avarice pushed harder.

She managed to get him into the bus. "Shut the door!" she screamed at the driver. And he did. Zip locked. Freeze dried. Airtight.

<22>

Avarice smiled limply, waved, and scurried away to prepare for an appointment at a salon where she would prepare for a trip to the pharmacy where she would prepare for a lunch at The Club where she would run amok amongst her peerless peers in all their Bergdorf Goodness.

Tears began welling up in Bryan's eyes. I fought to suppress them, needing to put an end to this spectacle. Outbursts drew attention, the last thing I wanted.

The driver jumped out of the bus and jogged after Avarice. They shared a few inaudible words, and she returned to the bus to recover Bryan.

< 2 3 >

FIVE

THE BACK OF the limousine was quiet. Quiet enough to think.

Obviously, I could not control Bryan completely. Even if I could, I wouldn't necessarily know what to do. My earlier incarnations acted on instinct, which affords a major advantage: instinct precludes decision-making. There are no choices. The guidelines are clear, unwritten and unspoken but undeniable. With instinct, one acts as one is supposed to all the time.

People, on the other hand, have diluted, repressed, and even outlawed their instincts. As a result, they have developed new and improved forms of dissociative behavior: confusion, delusion, denial, intellectual deterioration, and disorderly thinking. They are, as a population, schizophrenic.

I was chatting with a virus once. We were both be-tween hosts and got to joking about the "ability to reason," this grandiose notion people believe places them at the top of the pecking order. In fact, it plac-es them at the bottom because they have the "abil-ity" and yet still act as they do.

I knew a stingray named Manta who stung a man. I knew an electric eel named Falacee who stung a man. And I knew a man named Edison who electro-cuted an elephant, but Edison was no jellyfish.

"People," the virus summarized. "You can't live within 'em, and you can't live without 'em." He chortled. His laughter was infectious.

What was I just saying?

The limo was stopped at an intersection. I was gaz-ing west when next to us a shabby convertible rolled up. The car was a wreck, its body two-thirds rust, one-third primer, held together by the medallion of a stallion rattling on its left front quarter panel. The top was down, though from the dilapidated looks of it maybe it blew its top long ago, the stress of keep-ing its passengers safe with such a flimsy exoskeleton being more than it could endure.

How had that tattered old workhorse been spared the bullet this long? They usually put you down the moment you twist an ankle, much less after you've flipped your wig.

Two gentlemen rode in the front, a couple of set-tlers driving their carriage across the fruited plains,

<25>

or in this case, across the rust belt.

In the back seat was a young girl, not much older than Bryan. She seemed to be in heaven, floating on the wind of this sunny morning. She didn't care that her transport had no shell, that it offered no protection. As a matter of fact, she rejoiced in it, as free and unfettered as the ornamental horse glued to the side of that topless jalopy.

Bryan stared at her through the closed window. She was enchanting, with curly dark hair, pearly skin, and a constellation of freckles on her cheeks.

She noticed Bryan, too. In what appeared to be a friendly gesture, she stared right back. The two of them sat in their respective cars, observing each other for what seemed an eternity. Her face began to twitch, ever so slightly, as if she was fighting to suppress a smile. She lost.

Out came her teeth. They were large and white, a little crooked, with uneven gaps interspersed. The gaping holes in her smile made it all the more inviting. From the sheen of her hair and suppleness of her skin, I surmised she was a healthy specimen and her teeth would grow in nicely at some point.

She was safe, operating on one of my favorite frequencies, balmy and inspiring.

"Are you alone in there?" she said, as she scanned the vast expanse of our transport.

I could feel Bryan preparing a smile, and just as he was about to share it, a blinding stream of sunrise

<26>

struck the girl directly in the eyes. Her automobile rolled forward, made its turn, and continued on.

Quicker than she arrived she was, alas, gone.

<27>

SIX

IN THE CLASSROOM, Bryan jumped through all the flaming hoops. He stayed quiet, answered politely when spoken to, and kept his movements measured, in accordance with the others. He paid attention to both the teachers and students. We needed to be able to mimic their behavior in order to avoid arousing suspicion.

I closely monitored the airwaves for a friendly vibe. All I felt was pressure.

"Good morning, children. My name is Miss Power."

With a name like that I thought she may have been a distant relative of Earnie.

"Let's all stand and put our right hands on our hearts."

We obliged, except that Bryan was a lefty. So naturally he put up his left hand.

"Your right hand," Miss Power said. "Right hand."

We added the other hand, now running both hands around his torso searching for his heart, trying to appease Miss Power. But she only grew more frustrated.

"Right hand. On your heart. Right hand!"

Out of patience, she marched over, pinned his left hand to his side and held his right hand tightly against his chest.

"OK, everyone. Repeat after me. I pledge allegiance…"

It quickly became obvious that there in the nursery school is where domestication begins full-fledged, where they teach the sheep to pull the wool over their own eyes. Under the guise of molding upright citizens, they eviscerate their thought processes, dishearten their innate abilities, and send forth legions of unarmed, unprepared underdogs, steam-blowing tin men with something to prove and nothing to prove it with except a paper-thin degree of civility.

If you choose not to pledge, if you choke on the slogans, if you're not passively pasteurized, homogenized, and neatly poured into the carton of milk, you'll end up pictured on the side of it.

It would be tricky to navigate this minefield, to cheat the exanimation, to trudge through the tar pits without getting bogged down in the manufactory. But if I were to survive, we needed to do so.

Throughout the morning, while Bryan appeared

<29>

to watch and listen, I wandered out the window into the playground. It was mostly scrap metal, various apparatus smelted together in configurations designed to stimulate children's brains and provide an outlet for their spirited nature. As it was, it amounted to nothing more than a junkyard.

The monkey bars, however, had potential. They were high enough to separate us from the popping kernels and provide a vantage point where I could keep an ear out.

When the bell rang for recess, Bryan made a beeline for them and was at the vertex before I knew it. Below us, tribes, cliques, herds, and gaggles formed. And there was the occasional stray.

Sheppard Davis was the school bully. He was older than almost everybody for having been left back so many times. When he saw Bryan atop the monkey bars, the highest point in the playground, his superiority was threatened and he immediately advanced on us.

Monkey see monkey do, I suppose.

"Hey, twerp!" he squealed with glass-shattering annoyance, as he began his ascent. By the way he deliberately scaled the monkey bars, one could see that there was thought involved. He was fast, but he didn't know his body, or the bars, well enough to be completely fluid. It wasn't second nature. He was thinking, albeit quickly, and that made him slow.

He was considerably bigger than Bryan, and when

<30>

he perched himself opposite us it made me feel a little like Tom Thumb.

"Who are you, twerp?" he said, as he shoved Bryan. But Bryan held tightly, so Sheppard pushed harder. "Who are you?"

His intentions were clear. He was going to continue to ask rhetorical questions, which would provide an excuse to keep shoving until Bryan fell.

A crowd gathered in a sort of inverted coliseum, with the spectators below and the gladiators above.

That's where Sheppard's impure instincts failed him. He was imbued by the audience, invigorated by the thrill of the crowd. But flocks are fickle. The moment their illusions are shattered, they scatter. If Sheppard had been smarter, his instincts not already skewed by school, he'd have looked for courage not from the crowd, but from Bryan's fear. And if he took a look into Bryan's empty eyes, he'd have seen none, and would have perhaps desisted. But he was bent on having his moment in the rocket's red glare.

"You gonna answer me?"

As I remember it, Bryan used his solemn stare to pierce Sheppard's pupils, and then gave him one of the most brilliant answers I'd ever heard.

Sheppard was so perplexed I think he had an out-of-body experience, leaving his miscreant carcass prone to the elements. One of my favorite laws, gravity, took over from there and did our fighting for us.

< 31 >

Airship Sheppard hit the ground head first. The thud was echoed by a gasp from the crowd, now repulsed by what, a moment ago, they secretly longed to see.

A ways off, watching from outside the forum, was the girl from the convertible. She seemed unfazed, maybe even impressed, as she smiled again. Maybe it was her holey smile that brought down Bryan's competitor. Maybe she momentarily disrupted the atoms upon which he was surfing and he slipped through the cracks she'd created. I've seen stranger things.

Concussion, contusion, confusion. The stick figures gathered, manifesting a sense of urgency we didn't share.

<32>

SEVEN

EARNIE AND AVARICE were summoned to the headmaster's office, where Bryan tried to educate everyone in basic physics.

"It wasn't my fault he lost his grip," Bryan explained.

We all do, given the right circumstances.

"Every action has an equal and opposite reaction. He tried to push me. So there's the energy he used to push me, which I used to defend myself. Then I took into account the energy of activation, that energy which made him attack me in the first place. I think that's what knocked him down."

I'm surprised they didn't break out the Ritalin then and there. If they got a quick start on slowing him down, they wouldn't have to work so hard to keep up later. He was citing basic laws of nature,

ED RYAN

principles they were going to teach him in coming years. How much more concise of an explanation could they want?

I should have just said, "Might is Right!" Voila. A slogan. They love slogans. They'd have been saluting quicker than Pavlov's slobberers could fill a dribble cup. Cue the bright and fizzy, a flag and a breeze. All is forgiven.

"Even if this was an accident," the headmaster said, more to Earnie's wallet than to any person in the room, "and I'm willing to accept that it was, your son is, well…"

Weighing his next words carefully, he took in a deep breath and puffed his cheeks. He held it long enough for his face to tint red, and I hoped at that moment he had flossed.

"I think the other boy was bullying him. Don't you?" Avarice said, in her own strange way defending Bryan. She looked to Earnie for backup but he didn't hear her.

"It's not that," the headmaster said with a sediment-free exhale. "He doesn't…"

"Doesn't what?" Avarice barked.

The headmaster was walking a fine line, struggling to referee an internal grudge match between "think before you speak" and "say something before you look stupid." There was a long, pregnant pause. It is there, in those unplanned, muted moments, that the social defects gestate.

<34>

After all of nothing was said, Avarice buckled under the pressure of silence, and abandoned motherhood.

"You know," she stumbled. "He's not..." she fumbled. "Umm..." she umbled. Then she mumbled something into the headmaster's ear.

He had a clear reaction, as if one question ran off happily answered but an angry mob of others came knocking at his noggin. Information is funny like that. Not ha-ha funny. Peculiar funny. When one door closes, a dozen others open. Answers are nothing more than peat moss in a garden of perennials, forever sprouting new questions more brilliant than the one before.

The headmaster looked closer at the file, the manila envelope containing the paperwork. There's always the paperwork. You may as well be bar-coded at birth. Then he asked, "Bryan, how do you feel about staying here with us?"

To his credit, he asked the child's opinion. Maybe at some other time we could have been friends, he and I. But not now. It was better for us to be removed from the kerfuffle.

"I don't believe the school system will serve my needs."

So I left.

<35>

EIGHT

LIBERATED FROM THE lack of concentration camp, arrangements were made for home schooling.

Bryan breezed through any and all curricula as easy as A B Z. He went so quickly, in fact, that much of what they taught him went over my head, or through it.

I encouraged him to learn, but despite my best efforts he was not very interested in what they had to offer. He was more interested in me, the stories from my past, the lives I'd lived.

Bryan didn't share as much as I did. He seemed to have almost no memory of life before me. For all he knew, everyone had a silly little sylph behind their eyelids that kept them entertained, educated, and for my own safety, estranged.

The size of the estate afforded us the luxury of isolation. The main domicile had countless rooms for countless purposes: eating, drinking, cooking, reading, smoking. Quitting smoking. I don't know if we visited every one, but we could easily disappear for hours by ourself, just chatting.

The land surrounding the mansion was extensive as well, dozens of lush hectares. Much of its care was left to one of my favorite people, Bud the gardener. He tended dirt, of all things. He crawled in it, watered it, and fed it until it produced life. Then he tended to that.

No matter how far away, I could always hear him approaching. His vibrations were constant and comforting. Even when distressed or depressed, which was rare, he barely oscillated. He was grounded. Yes, that is the word for Bud. Grounded.

Bud had an extremely thick mustache which muffled his extremely thick accent. So thick in fact, his accent, that most people couldn't understand him, but I always seemed to catch his drift. Not that I was fluent in gibberish, but I'd heard enough of it to get by.

"Defense make good neighbor," he'd say, as we rode the perimeter of the estate on his little internal combustion vehicle. He was no dope. He just didn't sound like everybody else.

Bud's language barrier instilled in him plenty of patience. The simplest conversation with other people could drag on five times longer than necessary,

< 37 >

with all the repeating, rephrasing, and translating. We didn't fall into that claptrap. We listened, interpreted, and replied, or not.

Brevity. Lost on most.

He was very handy with a blade, too. He used a double-edged safety razor to splice plants together. Ingenious, as there is strength in diversity. I suppose that made him a botanist as well as a gardener. He probably formulated plants that needed less care and attention. This freed him up for other chores. He couldn't be there all the time for every leaf, stalk, and stem. It's a huge job, caretaker, too much to expect of one person.

What made Bud's botanical acumen even more impressive was how difficult it was just to pick up one of these razor blades, much less wield it with any accuracy. It's flexible and slippery, and so sharp you don't even feel it cutting your skin. The first time Bryan tried to pick one up, it made a bloody mess of his fingertips.

Bud conducted his horticultural experiments in the greenhouse, an artificially controlled environment protected by a layer of clear glass thinner than the hair on my chinny chin chin. It's also called a nursery.

In the nursery, nothing could go wrong. When outside was huffing and puffing, inside was just right. Whether outside was blisteringly hot or bitterly cold, inside was just right. You could be seeing

<38>

one thing while feeling something else entirely, like your signals were crisscrossed, like you were half in the body and half out.

Sometimes the weather became so tempestuous it threatened to blow the greenhouse down. You'd think this skinny shield could never withstand the pressure, that it would come crashing down like a counterfeit fairy tale with an unhappy ending. That's what you'd think, but you'd be fooled. That fragile aegis, she always held her own.

< 39 >

NINE

Bryan and I loved water, especially underwater. I didn't need to be a turtle to stay immersed for long periods. By minimizing physical exertion, you can decrease the need for oxygen to the point where you become virtually breathless. Down we'd go to the bottom of the pool, where we'd ponder, steep, and wonder.

Things are clearer there. What needs to be heard is heard. What needs to be blurred is blurred. And the ear-piercing fugue of confusion above is watered down to the soft impression of a sonic starry night.

This, like so much else, was considered odd and unnatural. What are pools to be used for? Cooking? People travel thousands of miles to go to Scuba, the underwater capital of the world. There are entire brochures devoted to it. I read them.

We paid for our love of underwater with chronic ear infections. They were painful and moody. Many of our hours were spent lying on a table with anti-bacterial ointment oozing around in his head. The relentless whoosh made me feel like a crab living inside a seashell.

There was a bright side to ear infections, however. They led us to Q-Tips. Whenever he needed to get water out of his ear, or if he just wanted to stop the whooshing, Bryan would rake them with a Q-Tip. Sometimes he'd dig so deep it felt like he was scratching my back. It was a delicacy we both savored.

A year or so after the nursery school debacle, Avarice tried once again to socialize young Bryan. She figured she'd use his love of water in her favor, to build on the momentum, as it were. She brought him to a public swimming pool. I'm sure she thought it was a good idea at the time.

The energy at the public pool was like every other popcorn machine, an assault on the senses. We jumped in and went straight to the bottom, in hopes of rendering tolerable the ruckus from the school of frolicking guppies above.

I don't know how long we were down there before the lifeguards blew their whistles, which underwater sounded like the trill of a Stradivarius.

Why all the fuss? There was no emergency. We were simply floating around in the middle of a conversa-

<41>

tion and wanted to be left alone. But the lifeguards, driven by the zeal to fulfill their summer oaths, dove in after us.

Bryan struggled to stay submerged as the two lifeguards pulled valiantly toward the surface. The fracas must have appeared quite out of order to those out of water, and in the melee Bryan's swimsuit was pulled off.

The great white cheeks breached the surface like Ahab's nemesis. Most everyone laughed. Avarice must have melted up into her wide-brimmed hat for the shame of it. His bare ass meant her embarrassment.

Parents Earnie and Avarice decided the time had come for some professional help. And they needed it. They were doing a horrific job. But that's not the kind of help they sought.

<42>

TEN

DOCTOR CHRIS was stenciled in thick black letters on the door. It was her shadow, I presumed, along with Earnie and Avarice's, which clouded the frosted glass encasing her fishbowl of an office. I thought I heard four voices, but I could see only the three watery figures.

We plopped ourself down on the couch, squarely in the middle of the well-worn path of least resistance, and waited patiently as our next chapter was being written for us in the other room.

I was all ears, listening carefully for you, or someone else like me, I mean, if here was where they brought people like us.

Our first impression of the white house was fear. But our fears were quickly allayed.

There were well appointed rooms, and the

grounds were well groomed, and the orderlies orderly loomed.

It was quite quiet. Soft colors and cushioned furniture with smoothly rounded edges muted any reverberation or dissonance. It was almost like being underwater, but I couldn't suspend reality that much.

Everyone was calm. They moved slowly, spoke quietly, and didn't look at you too closely, not into your eyes, anyway, which made me feel safe.

The man behind the counter, for instance, was dressed in snow white, clean and unstained. His clothes were cut perfectly, his hair coiffed curtly, and his teeth were whiter than Klansmen and straighter than Boy Scouts. His movements flowed like toothpaste, evenly and controlled. But I could tell he had a clear line, sharper than the crease in his pants, and anyone who stepped over it would be dealt with directly. If one, say, for instance, did dash for the door, flee for the freeway, or race for the razor blade, he would promptly overwhelm them with full, fluorinated force. But as long as you stayed on the correct side of the line, Mister Tartar Control was content to monitor his monitors.

A pang of angst poked me in the ribs. A girl had sat down beside us. Her skin was white with black stripes painted on, and her hair was dyed as black as Bryan's pupils. She had so much metal dangling from her leather jacket she could have safely jousted at the Renaissance Fair without donning any extra

< 44 >

body armor. I couldn't tell whether she was a new arrival, a recidivist, or checking out.

I wondered if those medals had been pinned to her jacket before it was killed, by some amateur matador. Or was it decorated posthumously, awarded the broken heart in the Vegetarian War?

An orderly approached and took custody of the jangling jacket, off to the funny farm, I suppose, to be treated for mad cow disease.

Zebra girl had what appeared to be hieroglyphics carved into her forearms. Bryan and I regarded them with fascination. She saw Bryan looking at her scars. The two caught eyes and looked at each other for a long time. I knew what she was thinking, and she must have known what Bryan was thinking, because we were all sitting there silently, getting along just fine. Then she so rudely interrupted.

"To keep my mind off the pain."

Her fingernails were clean, nicely manicured and fancifully painted. Obviously, she'd not used them to carve her distractions. It must have been a tool of some kind. I didn't really care.

Apparently the white house was a convalescence home for kids suffering from traumatic boredom, binge gilding, and a potpourri of other luxurious disorders. They were depressed, and happy to declare themselves so, torn between the desire to be different and the need to fit in. All this alienation was fashionably illustrated with tattered designer cloth-

< 45 >

ing, as frayed as their tortured young souls. I guess in order to rebel, you must properly accessorize.

Doctor Chris opened the door and invited Bryan inside. It was a heavy door requiring sturdy, well-oiled hardware. You wouldn't want to be next to it if it came unhinged.

We walked the linoleum plank. Even the floor felt cushioned, soft and padded with a slight bounce.

Avarice was wearing a hat and big sunglasses, trying to deflect attention. They weren't the same garments she'd worn at the pool, obviously. She'd never be seen in the same thing twice. It was against the rules, those ridiculous dictums she tried so hard to live by. She put herself through so much grief. For what? Who from the collagen committee was with her now, when she really needed a friend? And if one of her friends or neighbors were here on the grounds, it would not be to support Avarice. It would be to visit a kid of their own.

Earnie's hands remained deep in his deep pockets, but his heels bounced and his eyes wandered. He wasn't really interested in the surroundings or how they might help Bryan. He was putting a dollar cost average on this debacle, wondering whether Bryan, and perhaps Avarice, had reached the point of diminishing returns, whether he should just cut his losses now and be done with this whole family affair.

I liked them all better from the other side of the

<46>

glass, quiet and out of focus. If they could stay that way, muted and blurry, I might be inclined to tell the truth. It would be easier if they joined our dialogue instead of us joining theirs.

What if we did? What if we told them what was going on inside Bryan's head? Most likely they'd remain stone-faced and clear-eyed, appearing to listen. But with a free hand they'd be hitting the queasy button, the secret red panic enactor hidden under the desk. Just outside the frosty glass, the tubes of toothpaste would assemble. They'd storm through the doors, strap us down, and start drilling for cavities. Anything they did not recognize, anything unique, original, or otherwise out of the ordinary, would be considered decay and removed, replaced by some artificial composite or worse, simply left empty, unoccupied.

"Hello, Bryan. I'm Doctor Chris."

Like on the door? Unless, of course, you're using somebody else's office today. Good to know you have a firm grasp of the obvious.

She looked at Bryan patiently.

So…

She cast in a second line, fishing for a connection. "Do you want something to drink?"

You're going to need more than a Dr. Pepper, Dr. Chris, to boat my moat.

"He never talks," Avarice squawked, her sunglasses slipping askance.

<47>

She was wrong. He spoke. But seldom did he answer rhetorical questions. Why waste breath? Conserving air was part of our underwater regimen. And we didn't like to lie, which is what most words morph into the longer they linger.

"Never?" Doctor Chris replied, in what I perceived to be a lighthearted, perhaps even mocking, fashion. "Never ever?"

She wasn't trying to insult Avarice. She was trying to amuse Bryan, to lure him into letting his guard down by displaying, albeit gingerly, the type of mocking she'd expect of a rebellious child. She looked to him for a crack in the ice. What she got was an eyeful of emptiness. The problem with looking into Bryan's eyes was, you never got anything back. You only got lost.

"Well, almost never," Avarice backtracked. "Less than most other children anyway. He goes underwater, or into closets. He wanders. Wanders around the property."

Tour it. We tour the property, like any other tourist. Just because we don't carry a map doesn't mean we have no destination.

"Do you talk?" Doctor Chris asked him.

Bryan nodded yes.

"Shouldn't he answer?" annoyed Avarice asked annoyingly.

"When do you talk, Bryan?" the doctor asked, noting Avarice's imbalance, now trying more to calm

<48>

her than to reach Bryan.

I couldn't hold these cards forever. If we didn't say something soon, he'd look pretty crazy. Being mute can be dangerous too.

So he whispered, "Emergencies."

"What's an emergency?"

Ask Avarice. She's the one tapping out an S.O.S. with her fake fingernails.

"Was there an emergency at the pool?" Doctor Chris asked.

He nodded yes. "I lost something."

"What did you lose?"

"My bathing suit."

"The lifeguards pulled off your suit."

"Then you should be talking to them."

"They were trying to rescue you. It was an accident."

"Rescuing me was an accident?"

"You might have drowned."

"And they thought I should drown naked?"

Bryan didn't even try to hide the smirk on his face. I threw in the tilt of the head, another trick from the dog days of yesteryear.

"Well… of…" she stammered.

At a loss for words, Doctor? Welcome to my world.

<49>

ELEVEN

DOCTOR CHRIS'S PRESCRIBED treatment was three-pronged:

First, close the pools. Cruel and unusual, I thought, but the estate still had assets. Although underwater was my favorite sanctuary, I could work without it.

Prong two: quality time. She suggested to Earnie and Avarice they spend more time with Bryan. He was at a developmentally tender age and sound parenting was the best medicine.

Wrong again. A child's most developmental years are the first four or five, before I even arrived. What happened before then I can't attest to, but by age five or six, children are no longer tender. They are cooked.

As you might expect, the parents didn't delve too deeply into the quality time handbook, which may as well have been titled, "You, Me, and Ennui." They never made it past the first exercise in the first chapter: The Picnic.

The day started very nicely, in the limo. Maybe I was a little grumpy, having lost my underwater privileges, but we had ways of addressing moodiness. There was food and beverages, grass and games, a blanket and lots of sun. Earnie and Avarice were pleasant also. As the day progressed, they became even more cheerful, and eventually graduated to animated.

On the ride home, there was a half-eaten ham and cheese sandwich in the cooler, which had been cooking in the sun for the last few hours. The stench was pervasive, yet nobody mentioned it. They could have opened the windows, but that would allow the hot air in and the cold air out and start a calamitous cycle which could shatter the illusion of perfection. So that sandwich was going to have to sit there and rot, and we were going to deny it, and enjoy it.

If I were that sandwich, I'd want to be taken out and eaten. Once you're split in two, they may as well finish you off, right? You're already broken. Half of you has been devoured, the other half is expressing its anxiety by suffocating everyone in the limousine. Just get it over with.

Being chewed might not be so bad. If the teeth are healthy and enough saliva is added, it could be painless. But as I slid down the gullet, on my descent

<51>

into maelstrom, where there's always room for one more, the six thousand calorie question would be: how much of me will be properly digested and assimilated into the organism, and how much will be discarded as waste?

"Would you like something to drink, Bryan?"

"Pepsin."

"How about Coke?"

"Never mind."

You'd think with all their advancements in science and medicine, they'd have moved beyond "take two of these and call me in the morning." Yet that is still the pillar of medical treatment. The only difference is, the "two of these" used to be aspirin.

And that, my pharmaceutical friend, was prong three: mood enhancers. Anti-depressants. Psychotropics. Not the tropics I was interested in, certainly not the tropics where you'd find a place like Scuba.

Obviously we weren't about to introduce these dastardly drugs into ourself. We had enough to deal with already without having to hallucinate our way to sanity.

Bryan's parents, on the other hand, needed a hand. They drank a thermos full of cool aid, where I'd graciously stashed a week's worth of lucidity. Field tests corroborated the lab results. Mood enhancers work.

<52>

TWELVE

ONCE A YEAR, Mr. Crosson came to tune the piano. Most kids look forward to holidays, birthdays, and other occasions in which a social, historical, or spiritual fabrication provides cover for receiving tangible assets.

I had a different, though no less selfish, reason for loving my holiday. Tuning Day. It took me away, far from all that surrounded, confounded, and confined.

Bryan and I hid beneath the piano. I shouldn't say we hid, because we were in plain sight. But Crosson was stone cold blind. He didn't conceal his infirmity behind black lenses, which I found progressive. He forced the sighted to deal with him head-on, eye-to-eye.

They were a tough act to follow, Crosson's eyes.

They pin-balled unpredictably around his head in a pattern I could never chart. If you looked through his eyeballs, you'd probably see a tightrope walker tap dancing on his optical nerve. When he looked at you, it was like he saw everything around you: your aura, your energy, your guests. But not you. Who knows? Maybe he just had endo-vision. He saw inwards because his eyes had rolled over backwards.

Personally, I didn't care where he was looking or what he was looking for, as long as he supplied his annual antidotes. I don't even know how he got to the estate. He just seemed to arrive. But so did I, so who was I to question it?

As the conversations increased and the airwaves became more cluttered, crowding out at times even our own thoughts, the day of the tones meant peace of mind and clearness of conscience.

We crawled beneath the piano, perfectly positioned to absorb the vibrations. Crosson sat at the bench and administered his opiates, adagissimo, one by one by one, with the tempo and regularity of an intravenous drip. Every key keyed on the keyboard treated another symptom. The plangent tones resonated forever, undulating through Bryan's body, massaging his synapses, calming his mind, polishing our heart, and purring straight to my soul.

There, in the vibrations, is where we were together again, face-to-face, side-by-side, the child you are, the child I might have been, innocent, beautiful, po-

<54>

tential. Do you recognize me? It's easy to forget what one looks like after having been separated for so long. By now, I'm probably deep in the rear aisles of some remote warehouse, sleeping soundly in cache ZZ, buried in webs and bureaucracy. I wish I could go back and exorcise my narrative, undo all that tore us apart. But I cannot abandon the past any more than I can abandon my own mind, any more than the crew of a sinking submarine can abandon ship.

What of my parents? My real parents. Did they sob uncontrollably when given the grim news that I was missing, that my mission had gone terribly awry, and due to its secrecy all knowledge of me must be disavowed? For the longest time, I fooled myself into believing they would hound the hollow halls of justice with dogged determination until I was recovered. Suffice to say, I was wrong. But you? I know if you hear me, you will come. For us, there is still hope. As long as I can keep treading water.

<55>

THIRTEEN

ONCE, AS I floated upon the waves of the A, G, and C, imagining our reunion, I suffered a severe actual. I overheard a conversation. It was coming from far away, but not the outer-sphere. It emanated locally. If I was correct, if Bryan's ears were not deceiving us, it could mean trouble, real trouble. I had to forgo the remainder of my tuning that day and investigate.

Tracing the source led me to Earnie's office. There were three voices: Earnie, Avarice, and a voice from long ago, on speakerphone. It was the tour guide from the Galapagos. He'd tracked me!

Avarice had said taking the turtle was a serious matter. They probably wanted it returned. Were they going to cram me in that shell and ship me back to the wild? The Galapagos Islands were beautiful and a turtle shell is well and good, but Bryan served me far better.

I was not going to be taken away again. I didn't mind so much going to the white house. It was safe, quiet, and Avarice always came to pick me up. But back at the Galapagos, I didn't know who would come for me. The boobies? The lions? Warden?

That's when I tried to send the first distress call.

The concept was profoundly simple. I can't believe I hadn't thought of it before, but necessity is the mother of invention, and if one needs a mother it may as well be her.

Television, the two-pound test line binding an already flimsy social fabric. Bryan was often forced to sit in front of one. Hennessy only put me on a leash. This was worse, far more dangerous. But it is the broadest of broadcasters. Its signal is ubiquitous. If I could rewire one of the many we had on the estate into a transmitter, its power might reach you. Like me, you are always monitoring the airwaves whether you want to be, or not to be.

Sure, it was a half-baked plan, but lesser plans have been hatched. Remember Edison?

I needed a medium for my message, something simple but reliable. Simple always is reliable. More reliable than complicated, anyway. A device which could both record and play. Bryan already had one, but we never used it, of course. Speakers in the ears? Avarice gave it to him as a gift, but that fruity gizmo was digital, a technology as unstable as she. We

<57>

needed analog, an analog cassette player/recorder.

It would not be easy to find this defunct doohickey. I would need to scour electronics stores, houses of phosphor with walls of faces spewing immeasurable bytes of artificial intelligence. Any such foray would expose me to lethal levels of ambient din. It would be suicide, I mean real suicide, not these misconstrued faux pas we were constantly accused of.

To enter these chapels of babble, we'd have to have an attenuator. Not a helmet of plastic or metal. That would be ineffectual. The spectrum is too broad. Voices parry on far too many frequencies. Plus, a helmet begs attention and I couldn't afford to look like a typical loony. Bryan had a better idea.

We procured a wig from Avarice's vast collection. She had an entire closet full of them. I guess she was losing her hair, or pulling it out.

She should use the razor, like I did. Once you get the hang of it, it's easy, neat, and efficient.

Wigs are cushiony and thick. It would absorb the low frequencies. For the high frequencies, I used marbles. They are made of glass and agate, extremely hard materials, and they're round, the greater surface area providing greater refraction. We sewed them into sections inside a nylon mesh stocking and pinned that inside the wig.

Thus we invented the "meshagated headpiece," with marbles to reflect the high frequencies and the wig to absorb the lows. Everything in the midrange,

<58>

we'd have to deal with ourself.

As we should look more like a shopper than a shoplifter, the headpiece needed to fit unobtrusively. To that end, we needed to shave Bryan's head. We went to the greenhouse in search of Bud's razor. And that's when Bryan cut himself, the honest truth.

<59>

FOURTEEN

"WHAT DID YOU want with that razor blade?" Doctor Chris asked hospitably, way back when I thought she was hospitable.

It didn't look good, a young, introverted kid found with a blood-soaked razor blade in his hands. Of course, we couldn't fully explain what we were doing without revealing our plot. So we kept our answers.

Besides, once I was out of there, I was going to go back to the estate, shave Bryan's head, and proceed with the plan, which would almost certainly land me there again. I wanted to save some chat for then, you know?

Doctor Chris had an interesting vibe. It was a carrier frequency, a pilot tone, centered and stable. Around that maypole discharges frantically danced, leaping unpredictably from the left side of her lon-

gitudinal fissure to the right, like one of those elec-
trostatic generators in an old science fiction movie.
But it was not an organic tone, not native to her self.
It was a fabrication.

Was it a cure? Psychotherapists go through so
much treatment while they train. Maybe the years
of analysis, mantra, and meditation had sharpened
her skates so she could glide happily through countless hours of depressing dialogue with people with
people.

Or maybe she just nipped from the controlled
substances cabinet when nobody was looking.

I didn't envy her. She had to set the cadence for
an entire armada of yawing trawlers, goofy sloops,
loony schooners, and cowardly cutters, all vying for
an elusive space in her calming berth. That's a task
and a half.

"We're going to play a game," she said, turning
from a frontal assault to something more subversive.
"I'm going to say a word and you, you say the first
thing that pops into your head. Does that sound
fun?"

Did you major in psychology because you loved
it, or because it had the shortest line at registration?

"Ready? O…"

Oh come on, Doctor. Do you really think I inten-
tionally cut myself with razor blades? I wanted to
shave. It's not my fault clever Gillette designed such
a formidable defense mechanism. Other people mu-

<61>

tilate their bodies every day, with fake hair, fake lips, fake breasts, fake teeth, their skin supplemented for suppleness, suffused with base and rouge. They color, whiten, implant, extract, get simultaneously slimmed and plumped. Why are their excuses more acceptable than my explanation? I wouldn't be surprised if you've done a little mutilating yourself. If I listen carefully to your circulatory system, I hear a speed bump on your upper left shoulder. Upon closer examination, might we find a tattoo? A tiny lonesome teardrop, a monument to where your grade school girlfriends used to cry as you all complained about dateless nights and despicable parents.

It's not just your vibe that betrays you. I see much of your past right behind you. On the walls there are no family photos, and on your fingers there are no rings. By the smell of cheap, exotic spices, I surmise much of your free time is spent ordering international takeout food and scanning through cooking shows on your DVR. Instead of mincing meat and parsley on your chopping board, you mince and parse words with the likes of me.

Her decrepit method of slowing me down must have been working, because I only ran through the "O" words in the dictionary from "oaf" through "Oxford" by the time she finished her second syllable.

"…pen."

It didn't matter what she said and it didn't mat-

<62>

ter my reply. We could spend the entire week going through every dictionary in every language. My reason for wanting the razor blade was simple.

"Occam."

<63>

FIFTEEN

UNFORTUNATELY, ANALOG IS more outdated than you'd imagine. We scoured chain stores, malls, and department stores, to no avail. We must've looked pretty normal, though, because nobody took note of us.

As the day dragged on, interference began to bleed through. This should have been expected as the headpiece was only a consumer model, not designed for industrial strength shopping. I didn't know how many more sorties it was good for. We were losing focus, daylight, and sight of our pot of gold.

The end of the rainbow turned out not to be an electronics store at all. It was a quiet, non-descript shop somewhere out on the island, antique I believe, or pawn. Peeking into the front window, I could see there were not a ton of TV's turned on, so I thought it probable we'd survive this one last incursion. I aligned the headpiece, took roll call of our faculties, and entered.

We were immediately pummeled by a blast of low-level X-rays from a security scanner. It should be no surprise this mom and pop shop would spring for a scanner. Large and small, everyone everywhere is big in security. Bryan leaned his entire body forward and plunged through the invisible wall.

We walked along the display counter towards the proprietor at the far end. He was a rotund sort, egg-shaped, with a waistline longer than his inseam. He did not take notice of me until I spoke.

"Garcon," I said.

His humpty head spun ninety degrees in my direction. His dumpty body held fixed, not moving a single degree.

I said something else, to which he aligned his trunk with his dome and waddled towards me, ticking to and tocking fro, like a slow-mo metronome. When he finally arrived, I told him what I needed, something that both played and recorded.

"Analog," I specifically specified.

He acted like he knew what I was talking about and, moving as few muscles as possible, reached into the glass cabinet between us and produced a digital device.

"Analog. Tape," I said, already feeling like my wig was beginning to leak. "Do you know what I'm talk-

<65>

ing about?"

"A tape deck?"

How does he stay in business?

But that's not why I started scratching my head. The nylon portion of the head piece was irritating Bryan's freshly shorn scalp, whose skin had become very sensitive from exposure, a design flaw I did not foresee. We needed to pick up the pace.

I spotted something high on a shelf behind the counter. "There, there. Please."

It was a bright yellow device, no larger than a wallet. It had four letters stenciled on but I don't know what they stood for.

As if he was doing me a favor, he rolled a wooden ladder into place, lumbered up a few steps, pulled the dirty package from the wall, and with his three free limbs, grappled down the creaking rungs. His return journey to the cash register was a wheezing epoch, his waddle gone catawampus from the eleven ounces of added ballast.

I grew seasick just watching him, like we were standing on opposite ends of a diving board.

Not recognizing his own merchandise, he examined the package from every angle, looking for a price tag.

"That's funny."

"It's really not."

"Muddy," he called to the back. "Muddy," he said louder, trying to summon the great appraiser, but no

<66>

muddy appeared.

A fly landed on my cheek and I swatted it, only to realize it was not an insect at all, but a bead of sweat from Bryan's irritated scalp, followed shortly by another. The plan was unraveling. Bryan's synapses were beginning to palpitate.

"Just improvise, something between a piece of junk and a collector's item," I said. "I don't care."

"I don't want to cheat you," I think he said. "Let me see if I have another." And he headed back toward the ladder.

The itching became unbearable. We were moments away from ripping the headpiece off and scratching Bryan's brains out. I reached over the counter, pulled the device from the proprietor's hand, and headed for the door. Bryan may have dropped some money or a credit card on the counter, but for all I know it was a robbery.

I could hear the X-ray scanner revving up. It was going to be more difficult getting out than getting in. We diverted all our energy forward, closed our eyes, and damned the torpedoes, full speed ahead.

We blasted through the X-ray wall with ease. The glass door, however, was not as penetrable.

<67>

SIXTEEN

"As you can see, I have some cards here," Doctor Chris said underhandedly, back before I thought she was underhanded.

The Rorschach Test was a move up to what I thought at the time was the big guns. Little did I know she had an ace up her sleeve, a larger repertoire than I gave her credit for.

"On these cards are patterns."

"Pictures?" Bryan asked.

"Yes."

"Like postcards?"

"Sort of."

"From where?"

"I don't know."

"What's the picture of?"

"That's what I want you to tell me."

"You're already looking at it."

"Yes."

And you need me to tell you what it is? Why is this place so expensive, other than the electric bill?

"OK. Ready?" she asked.

At first I was giddy with anticipation, but as she turned the card I got bored. And you know what they say about an idle mind.

"A tat…"

"Bryan, you need to give me a second to turn the card around. Then you look at it and tell me what you see. OK?"

UGH! She was still turning the card! And I thought turtles were slow. I couldn't take any more. I was fine when I got here, but now she was making me want to kill myself.

"What do you see?"

Finally.

"A tattoo. A teardrop. On someone's back," I said, without even opening my eyes.

Her vibe went as crazy as an Irish melody. I shivered her timbers.

Don't leave me, Commodore. I'm sorry. Please, give me a second chance.

"OK." She cleared her throat. "Let's do another." She shuffled up a second card. "And when you look at this, what do you see?"

We looked at it with all the interest we could feign. What I saw was a black card with uneven white edg-

<69>

es, more boring than I could have imagined. Bryan furled his brow, trying to look inquisitive.

"The first thing, Bryan."

I wanted to give her something good, a big, fat, juicy gift she could sink her training into. If she was happy, I was two.

"What do you see?"

"Blood," I said. "Lots of blood, running from my wrists."

She must have liked that answer, because she kept him for a while.

<70>

SEVENTEEN

To ENSURE PRIVACY, Bryan's parents rented an entire hallway in the main building of the white house just for him. I don't know what happened to the other patients who had been residing there. Maybe they were given placebos and sent home.

We now had express check-in, no more waiting in line, just walk past the toothpaste man and go straight to our room. Believe me, my Freudian friend, to earn those types of perks at such an exclusive club, you have to accumulate a lot of freakwent flier miles.

As a home away from home, the white house was a halfway decent place. In many ways it was like the estate, though not as large. Bud could have caretaken it in his sleep. Heck, he could have carved a miniature of it and put it in a bottle. There were lovely gardens, serene walking paths, and a mollifying ambiance. There was even a chapel, for those who needed to hyperextend their survival instincts another twelve steps.

And I thought this place was intended to cure diseases of the mind, not instill them.

Savior self.

It was kismet that Bryan's head was already shaved, because Doctor Chris developed an innovative treatment method I'd never heard of. She put tuning forks to Bryan's head and generated tones, lovely low frequencies that just sort of hummed peacefully, like a pacemaker for the brain. It was quite pleasant, and did manage to put Bryan on a better wavelength. I rather enjoyed it myself.

At first.

<72>

EIGHTEEN

Every year Crosson had less hair on his head, except in his ears, where it grew thicker, which I suppose in the strictest sense is on his head. But you know what I mean. Or you should.

Eventually, what follicles survived went from tricolored: black, gray, and graying, to monochromatic, all gray. Where he lost color in his hair he gained it in his teeth, which had gone yellow, and on his skin, where brown blotches grew larger and, to be honest, a bit unsettling. None of this had any effect on his tuning procedure, however, which was still an elixir.

In the last two years, I could tell by the sound of his touch that he had a guest of his own. A most uncompromising, unwelcomed accompanist had landed a regular gig in Crosson's joints. Rheumatoid

Mary. Yes, Miss Arthritis had been crowned queen of his skeletal system, and every day she repeated the same routine in the talent contest, that old standard, degenerative pain. But Crosson was a merry old soul, and the show went on. Although I could hear the torment in his knuckles, it didn't transfer to the keys, which were forever dulcet.

I usually left the room before he reached the higher keys. Those notes in the upper register were painful. I was just about to decamp one day, the only day, when Crosson spoke.

"Hey, man."

"Huh?" I started, taken aback by the sudden acknowledgement. All these years he must have known I was there. He was no dope. He just didn't look like everybody else.

"What are you still doing here?"

I didn't really understand his question, but I didn't want to leave him in the dark. So I gave him a stock reply.

"I don't know."

"Aren't you gettin' kinda old?"

"Almost twelve."

"I see."

Um…

"You're that one that graduated from college so young, right?"

"That I am."

"Why don't you go away? To school?" he asked.

<74>

"Why don't you ever play songs?" I retorted. I felt like poking him in the eyes. But what good would that do?

"I don't know any."

"Couldn't you learn them?"

"Notes are prettier. Don't you think? When you start making chords, it gets cluttered."

"Like voices."

"Who needs a triad?"

"Three's a crowd."

"You could say," he chuckled. "If I was deaf, it would be different, right? Then I wouldn't hear all the other noise, and maybe I could enjoy the melodies. But unfortunately, I'm just blind."

"I see," I said. We both laughed.

"You're damn smart," he continued. "You gotta go out in the world and do great things."

"Isn't what I've already done great enough? It's more than anyone else ever does."

"You could find a cure for cancer."

I started to explain to him a formula I was developing, like a theory of relativity, which involved increasing life expectancy, the average rate of cell division, random selection, financial determinism, and the business of cancer. Then I just said, "It's more preventable than curable."

"I see."

"Um, do you?"

"What?"

"See."

"No."

"That's more curable than cancer."

"Ah," he said. And he leaned down towards me. He seemed to know my exact coordinates because he came within inches of my face. The tuner's spastic eyes rolled around in their sockets, each in a different direction, drawing me in like a spinning spiral, or pulling me out like a corkscrew. I was losing my bearings. I shut my eyes to fend him off, but he leaned right into my ear and murmured, "Go awaaayyy…"

His voice was as hypnotizing as his notes. It was the closest I ever came to giving up the ghost.

Now I know where sound goes when it dissipates. Never mind Doppler. It's Crosson. He knew the secret to peace and quiet.

That was the first I ever spoke with Crosson, and the last. He died a few months later, blindness being his only reward. I hope he is well.

Nobody ever returned to tune the piano. That was almost a year ago.

< 76 >

PART II

NINETEEN

I REMEMBER THE day I heard Avarice say, I remember it like it was, yes, today.

"Congratulations, Bryan. You've been accepted to…"

Some or another U.

Accepted at a university? We didn't even apply.

The mistake I made was letting Bryan excel. In so doing, he stood out. We'd done what was asked, many times over, and I thought they would leave us alone. But it was just the opposite. They wanted more.

Attending a prestigious school for an advanced degree at such a young age would draw attention. Inquisition would follow. They'd put him on stage in front of cameras, to be paraded around like Frankenstein or King Kong. If ever we faltered, they'd turn up the voltage and send me off to rendezvous with Topsy. Or worse, he'd become an exhibit at Animal Kingdom or some other vacuum-packed habitat, on the wrong side of the glass at the Museum of Natural History.

Universities were pleased and eager to accept a young prodigy into their graduate programs, especially one with a lineage capable of making such sizable contributions. His parents were just as eager to send him away.

Bryan had become the 800-pound gorilla riding the white elephant. Any semblance of family life had evaporated long ago. Earnie and Avarice relinquished hopes of being parents and instead focused on keeping up appearances.

This latest advancement in higher education would satisfy community standards and get Bryan out of the house. From there, he'd be pushed to even higher educations and institutions, where he'd be beaten into submission by degrees. There was no avoiding it this time. They were determined to send him away.

I dusted off my old playbook, with one massive modification.

<80>

TWENTY

ONCE UPON A time, we'd attended a dinner way up-stairs at Thir-D Rock Plaza in New York City, the communications capital of the world. It was some-body's birthday and Bryan's parents needed him to help simulate a family. Or maybe it was Bryan's birthday. I don't remember. I never knew his exact birthday. It was never celebrated with much convic-tion. Sometimes on a Tuesday the seventh. Some-times on a Thursday the ninth. It was like singing "Auld Lang Syne." Nobody knows the words or what they mean. They just know they're supposed to sing right… about… now!

Bryan didn't mind. And neither did I. It wasn't my birthday, or my parents.

Imagine, though, if everyone with the same birth-day formed a country. There would be 365 diverse countries and everyone would have something in common, other than borders.

Atop this plaza, there was a ginormous broadcasting facility. They had the power. They had the antenna. And they had tours!

The old analog device was still recorded and ready to go, as simple and reliable as ever. I would join a group, sneak away to the roof where the power source and antenna were surely located, hook up, transmit, and return before anyone noticed me missing.

I know what you're thinking. Dangerous can't begin to describe a journey to the center of the dearth. We may as well go bobbing for apples in a barrel full of hungry piranha. The first visit to Thir-D Rock Plaza, for the aforementioned birthday, fell on a Tuning Day so I was prepared, fit as a fiddle. This time, however, I'd have to rely on my resistance training.

As the frequency of my visits to the white house increased, so too did the frequency of the tuning forks. Doctor Chris had gone Edison on me. The last time we were there, she hit notes even Crosson couldn't reach on his piano, so high they sent Bryan into convulsions.

I'll bet there's nothing in the brochure about that! Seeking asylum, I burrowed deeper into his psyche, but I couldn't escape the tremors. Like any self-respecting, self-preserving creature would, I developed a defense mechanism. I hummed ohms and notes over and over, until I phased everything out.

<82>

Ohms and notes. Ohms and notes.

What was I just saying? Thir-D Rock.

Ticket in hand, I waited for the next departure. I needed a distraction, something to focus on, so I grabbed a discarded Tuesday newspaper. It said something about a dinosaur, a fossil or other artificial fact.

Before long my group was called and, single file, herded through a turnstile. The insidious contraption clicked loudly with each rump it rubbed, clicking and clicking, louder and louder, a torture rack stretching my nerves into confession. Distant whispers crept in, questioning the perspicuity of my plan.

Are you now, or have you ever been, a member of a television studio audience?

If this was any indication, Bryan's head might explode on the elevator ride up.

"Ohm. Ohm. A G and C."

Having second and third thoughts, I tried to retreat, but it was too late. I was ensnared in the clutches of the groping grinder. Two of its three arms were wrapped around my thighs, driving me forward.

"Hey. You," a voice said. One of the tour guides began walking in my direction, approaching with all the purpose of a poacher. Naturally, I thought I'd done something wrong and was about to be reprimanded. Then she smiled, flying the flag of friendship.

That is something to which I would pledge alle-

<83>

giance.

Lo and behold, it was the girl from the car, the one who watched Bryan on the monkey bars, the one we'd seen many times here and there and here again. The one who was constantly appearing, disappearing, and reappearing over the years. Her teeth had come in nicely, just as I'd expected

Slowly I calmed, with the help of her balmy vibe.

"You used to live down the street from me," she said. "We went to school together. You beat up Sheppard Davis on the monkey bars."

"It wasn't really a fight."

We just showed him the quickest way down.

"It totally was," she said. "Didn't you get expelled for that? Cuz you pretty much totally disappeared."

"Yeah, well, we traveled a lot."

Which we didn't. Bryan didn't have a passport, or birth certificate for that matter, none that I'd ever seen. Among the mounds of paperwork, the envelopes, the transcripts, the EEGs and EKGs, there was no birth certificate. Nothing official, set in stone, that showed who he was or where he came from. Even dinosaurs a million years dead have a better idea of when they were born.

"Didn't you graduate college when you were like, two?"

"Times five point five."

"Huh?"

"Eleven. I got a bachelor's degree when I was elev-

<84>

en. Last year."

"That's amazing."

She was a finer specimen than Bryan. Her posture was perfect and her musculature was proportionate to her bone mass, giving her a sturdy stride. She was not exceptionally tall, but her spine was erect, aided by strong abdominals. She spoke from her diaphragm, the way one should, and her voice was one of the most pleasant sounds I'd ever heard.

She was from estate row, too, though not from a mansion. Her family inhabited a more modest house, and had moved from there a few years ago to make permanent residence somewhere upstate. She was working this summer to help pay for an all-girls boarding school she would attend in the autumn. She had a Band-Aid on her arm, which she got from a blood bank. She donated every week.

Much to my surprise, she continued the conversation.

"What did you major in?"

Like I said, he'd studied so many different things, most of it went in one ear and out the other.

"This and that."

"Well then, what was your favorite thing to do?"

"Writing."

Bryan? He never told anyone of his writing. Not even his tutors.

"What kind?"

"Fiction. Not for the news, just short stories and

<85>

poems."

"What're you doing here?"

"I don't know. Just thought I'd see the sights."

"Here?" she whispered. Then she mussitated, "Boring."

Normally by this point, my mind would have wandered and I would have stopped listening. Not from rudeness or anything. It was just, well, between Bryan and me, there was always someone else to talk to and something else to think about.

"I'm Connie."

"Con Me?" Bryan quipped. It was very unlike him to be so casual with a new acquaintance, but we were in complete accord. She was safe.

She smiled and said dryly, "Ha ha. Connie." Then she said something that was arresting: "Short for Constants. Constants O'Really."

Constants: things that do not vary or change. Constants.

I think I like that.

<86>

TWENTY-ONE

As THE BUTTERFLY would have it, Connie wanted to show Bryan the Chelsea Hotel, because of all the famous people who had stayed there, especially writers.

Bryan, being a writer, should see it. It, being a landmark, should be seen. And I, being almost gone, should have opted out. But if I was going to be leaving him, he needed to have other friends, and this seemed a good place to start.

The heat that summer was the worst I'd ever experienced. Swollen sidewalks came up to greet your feet, but there was no wind at your back. Despite the suffocating Celsius, we walked to the nearest subway.

Constants recalled the many times the two of them had seen each other but never spoken. They wondered how they could have lived so close, yet never met. The answer is simple: he is a member of the idle class, she the working. Seldom do they mingle. But it would have been rude to say it out loud so the truth went unspoken, as it so often does.

On the sidewalk near the subway station a crowd had gathered, listening to a man angrily ranting into a microphone. He was drastically over-modulating his under-powered sound system. The distorted volume caused the hammers in Bryan's eardrums to pound with such ferocity, I half expected them to start bleeding, which would then trickle around inside his ear and drive me crazy.

What the yeller lacked in clarity, he compensated for in gesticulation. His jabber was vitriolic, devoid of credible content, but he garnered attention because he was LOUD!

I pushed through the annoying Barnumites and found my way to the subway station, hastily seeking quietude in the underground.

Just outside the entrance, I saw a waterless fountain. Parched from the intense summer sun, its cracking pipes protruded from the tiled concrete. Schools of pedestrians passed the dehydrated fountain without heed. They'd listen to the blaring shrill from the odious toad, but pay no attention to this urgent warning. I wanted to grab the microphone and point it out. But proceed with caution when you're denying denial. The torch-bearing village idiots will throw a hood over your head and whisk you away

<88>

quicker than they shrouded Turing.

Drought. They know it's coming, but why worry? There are substitutes for everything: vitamins, minerals, physical activity. They've already begun decreasing their reliance on water, oxygen, and nutritive sustenance, devolving along with the mother planet they're destroying, so when it can no longer sustain them they won't need it anyway.

Maybe, my photosynthetic friend, they are shrewder than I thought.

Down we went, from the merely sweltering to the melting.

<89>

TWENTY-TWO

THE SUBWAY TUNNEL reminded me of my brief stint as an ant. It's no small feat being an ant. The world rested on our shoulders, ours and worms'. We were building the foundations of the earth, not some dinky little business or brand. With so much responsibility and only twenty-four hours in a day, we did what any diligent species would: we invaded other ant colonies and took slaves. We didn't see anything wrong with it. We were ants. I don't condone it. Slavery is an ugly thing, but I never knew an ant with a logo on its shell.

A few stops on, the train experienced trouble so we had to ascend at 34th Street and walk.

It's difficult holding a conversation on the crowded sidewalks of the garment district, we and Constants constantly weaving in and out of oncoming traffic, jockeying for position against racks of clothing. But we managed.

Ouch!

Nearing the hotel I felt something was amiss. Almost as soon as I noticed I was enjoying myself, I was struck by a sense of impending doom. Everyone seemed to be looking at Bryan as if they were looking for me, and just when they were out of sight they would grab the nearest phone and call the proper authorities.

"You want something to drink?" Connie asked.

"Water."

She went into a deli, leaving Bryan to admire the outside of the hotel. I felt like it was sending me messages, or warnings. It could have been residual vibes from its earlier guests, the many lives lived and lost, whose echoes still resonated.

No, something was trying to tell me someone.

Earnie came gamboling out the front door with a grin on his face, the Cheshire Cat of the Chelsea Hotel. He had not seen Bryan yet, but they were on a collision course.

Much to my surprise, Bryan stood still, making no effort to evade him. I, on the other hand, wanted no part of any phony familial farce. I considered cloaking but there wasn't enough room around Bryan to go dervish.

"Ohm. Ohm. A G and C."

They bumped into each other and froze, face to

<91>

face. A deafening silence drowned out the urban din, and another in a lifetime full of long, pregnant pauses befell us.

I was certain either Earnie or Bryan would look away, but Bryan felt to do so would forever bury the chance of a proper greeting he and Earnie never had, and hasten the farewells they probably never would.

There was a strange sensation deep inside Bryan, deeper even than where I resided, that he actually hoped for some sort of scolding, a stern reminder that he shouldn't be wandering the streets of New York without alerting his parents. And if Earnie really wanted to stretch the envelope, he'd insist Bryan come home with him this instant. And Bryan would have obliged.

The moments became mitotic. As Earnie hawed and hemmed, the garment district came to mind, an incident that was so quick it should have been forgotten.

Pushing through the crowd, Bryan's hand had smacked knuckle-to-knuckle with a passerby. It hurt, a lot. Through all that clamoring indifference, this woman and Bryan reached out, clasped each other's hands, made direct eye contact, and simultaneously exclaimed, "Sorry." Then they released hands and were washed away in the grim river of humanity.

No such contact between this father and son would be made today. As Earnie fidgeted, a pigeon on the

<92>

sidewalk came strutting along. Personally, I don't like those birds. They are a nuisance and public health hazard. They say there's little difference between pigeons and doves, but they're not always right. Maybe they tested only the lab specimens and not the birds on the street. That's usually where the problems with theories occur, in their actualization. Everything works fine on paper. But once you take it out of the test tube, a separate life develops, unplanned and unpredictable. So I would have to disagree. I think there's a big difference between pigeons and doves. The woman whose hand we smashed into, she was a dove. A lovely dovely.

Theoretically, Earnie should have done the talking. He was the adult. But something was becoming clear. Earnie was more befuddled than Bryan was. It sounded like he had a tourniquet around his lungs, like he was on a respirator. It is the sound of deception, and I knew any word uttered at that moment would fail the laugh test for honesty.

Much to my amazement, he ambushed us, foiling my meager expectations with a totally honest statement. I wasn't sure whether he was cunning and adroit or oblivious and asinine, but what he said was absolutely true.

"I haven't seen you at dinner lately."

His inadvertent candor was the beginning, middle, and end of an unapologetic, anti-child-rearing pamphlet, and it drove a stake through the heart of

<93>

any hopes Bryan may, or may not, have had for even a semblance of a father-son exchange.

Bryan's heart fell into his stomach. Fortunately, I was there to catch it. I replaced it without missing a beat. I don't think he even noticed.

Other than that, Earnie had nothing erstwhile to say. So he left.

A moment later, Connie returned with two waters. "Here you go."

Bryan took his without saying a word.

"It's beautiful, right?" she asked.

"What is?"

She nodded toward the hotel.

"Uh huh," he replied, half lying. He lifted the polyethylene bottle to his lips and sipped. I reluctantly obliged.

<94>

TWENTY-THREE

THERE ONCE WAS a planet named Pluto. It lived on the edge of the solar system. One day, a decision was made that Pluto would no longer be a planet. It was deemed unworthy because it was too small, or too far out. Demoting a planet is an immense move with inter-galactic consequences. Who gets to make such a decision? Is there some sort of symposium? An election? A Parliament of Astronomers? Or is it just the Napoleonic chairman of Planned Planethood?

Why can't they leave well enough alone? All the minds that knew and loved Pluto as the ninth planet had to scramble to reorient themselves, to re-learn everything from scratch. And you know what happens when one goes back and re-examines what they've been taught? They realize most of it is false. There follows an era of intellectual anarchy or, as I like to call it, freedom.

Neither Earnie nor Avarice ever uttered a word about the circumference of Bryan's orbit.

<96>

TWENTY-FOUR

THE FOLLOWING WEEK, I saw Connie at the blood bank. We had made plans to meet for an afternoon promenade. Did I mention the first time I met her, at the turnstile, she had a Band-Aid on her arm? It was from donating platelets, which she did routinely, every week. She didn't take any money. She did it simply to do the right thing.

I was carrying my recording in the hopes I could steer our afternoon to the broadcast facility. I figured with her privileges, she could get me access to the roof, and maybe even show me to some restricted areas. I wanted to start broadcasting as soon as possible. It was anyone's guess how long it would take you to receive my message. I also figured her calming energy would guide me through the area without incident.

Arriving early, I sat in the waiting room, prepared to fend off the inevitable assault on my senses. A cranky old air conditioner hung precariously in the window, clinging to shards of cracked Plexiglas and duct tape, buzzing steadily, much like Doctor Chris's carrier frequency. I latched onto it and re-occupied my mind.

For a group of people about to be lanced, there didn't seem to be much tension in the air. I did hear a few fidgety donors, the fabric of their garments scraping against the plastic, institutional chairs. Cotton slid easily, as opposed to gabardine, which was also soft but the resistance of the twill weave is scratchy. Polyester was harsh, as you'd expect plastic on plastic to be. Silk was the softest, but it is expensive. Most rich people don't give blood. They take it. We didn't hear much silk at the blood bank.

I opened my eyes to see Connie outside, striding toward the door. She grabbed the handle and pulled but it didn't open. She had husky arms, and summoned her upper body strength for assistance. When the door opened, the sound of it scraping the metal saddle was abusive, needles in my ears.

Connie's archless All-Stars squeaked on the floor. It was a very high pitch also, but her rubber soles seemed musical. She was wearing a short, airy dress, cotton, a wise choice, most forgiving to her skin in the merciless heat, and easy on my ears when she sat down.

<98>

Why every head in the room did not turn to see her is beyond me. They will look at a stone wall or a painting with a disfigured face and say they are beautiful. They create abominations, pyramids and sphinxes, laying waste to perfect space, and call them wonders of the world. But a true original goes unnoticed and uncelebrated.

A moment after she crossed the threshold, Miles, her brother, followed. Over the years, I'd seen him from a distance, but we had never formally met. He was the one in the front of the convertible that day Connie and I first saw each other.

Just as Miles entered, the brown, suffering air conditioner kicked into overdrive, groaning with dissatisfaction. Already on life support, it was begging to be retired. But when you get your amps from donations at a blood bank, whose profit margins are razor thin, there's no real money for an upgrade, so that old A.C. was just going to have to get its Freon.

"Hey, Bryan," Connie said, smiling, her wintry white face glistening with perspiration, those freckles dotting her cheeks where the snow had melted. "You ever hear of a cell phone?"

"Yeah. You know…"

"Are you one of those afraid of the radio waves?" she asked. "Like they get in your head and fry your brain?"

"Yes!" I said, excited to no end.

"You don't believe that stuff, do you?"

<99>

"Well, there is some science to it."

"That it causes brain damage?"

"Maybe not in everyone."

"Only people with weak brains," she said proudly.

"You'd think he had one in both ears," Miles threw in under his breath, as if Bryan couldn't hear him.

"Get a smart phone," she advised Bryan, trying to deflect her brother. "You don't need to talk on it. Just text."

"They don't work," Bryan said.

"What? Texts?"

"Smart phones."

"Dur. Very funny," she said. Her sarcasm was honestly refreshing, non-toxic, unlike her brother.

"Have you two ever met?" Connie asked.

"Hey," Miles said, with a suspicious demeanor.

"We used to live down the street from him. Remember?"

"Yeah, I remember him," he said, with no more enthusiasm than his first grunts.

Connie continued, "So we can give blood, mwhah-hah, and then maybe have some lunch or something? Is that OK with you, Bryan?"

"Let's head back to the TV station. We never made it to the roof."

"Dude, it's my day off," she said.

"Why don't we go to the zoo?" Miles said out loud, then whispered to her, "They like zoos."

She swatted him.

<100>

Who was he not talking to? Did he honestly think Bryan couldn't hear him, or that he wouldn't understand his witticisms? And I use that term loosely.

"How are your folks there, buddy?" Miles asked. "Doing alright?"

No matter what he said or how he said it, he was offensive.

"Fine," I replied.

"Still on the island?"

"The long island."

"It must be tough living like that, drowning in all that money. I don't know what I'd do."

"Try not to breathe."

He didn't get it. She did, and quickly shoved him over to the reception desk to sign them in. Miles had to vouch for Connie, as she was a minor and he a dolt.

After the blood bank, we went to a museum. Inside was dark and cool, a welcome reprieve from the relentless summer. Constants was a welcome reprieve, too. She was genuinely kind to Bryan and treated him with sincerity, which was a nice change from most others. We made her laugh. That was also a nice change from simply amusing ourself. Sometimes she spoke slowly, in a cautious monotone, like she was trying to keep from startling him. It may have been the difference in their ages. For teenagers, a few years can be a chasm.

Despite the climate control, I wasn't comfortable

<101>

at the museum, sort of out of sorts. People gander and meander for hour after hour, staring and glaring with "oohs" and "ahhs" and "blah blah blahs" while they digest the dioramas of Natural History or dissect Dada at Moma.

For Bryan's sake, though, I was willing to help him develop an appreciation of art and such. If all went well, I'd be gone soon, and he needed to have something in common with other people. He needed hobbies. Hobbies and friends.

<102>

TWENTY-FIVE

DURING ONE OF my stays at the white house, I can't recall which, they seemed to fuse together after a while, there was a massive electrical storm, as violent and scary a weather system as I'd ever seen. It rattled the windows and walls of the buildings, and the nerves of its occupants, especially mine. Some days later I went back to the estate.

Together, Bud and I surveyed the grounds for storm damage. It was fairly extensive. Around every turn were bent bushes and tilted trees. Most other guys would have brought in tractors and bulldozers to replace or replant the exiled shrubbery. But not Bud. He did not seem overly concerned with what he saw.

"Not too bad," he said, understanding perfectly well that, "Things have a way they go, yes?"

"Yes," I echoed. "Away they go."

We continued to ride on Bud's little vehicle until we came upon a gaping hole in the sky. There once stood the tallest tree on the estate, the skyscraper of the tree line. It had been split violently in two, probably a direct hit by a bolt of lightning. The roots were still firmly in the ground but the trunk had tumbled sideways, off axis, clinging to the base by a few sinewy strands.

I loved that tree. It was one of the most remote sanctuaries, a place I often went looking for you. Bud loved it, too. When he saw the destruction to the thick trunk, his frequency wavered, his lips quivered, and the late September wind dragged a tear down his stubbly cheek. I hadn't seen him so distraught since the time he told me of his wife.

Bud had been married, but his wife died long ago. He blamed himself for not emigrating from their homeland sooner, where medical care was lacking. Maybe if she had lived and they'd had a family, he would have cared for them like he cared for the estate. That would have led him in a different direction, to another profession like a plumber or banker, and he'd have focused his nurturing nature on his kin instead of mulching and leeching.

I hated seeing Bud so out of tune. I could feel it myself, like he was wired right to me. I needed to steady him before we both lost balance.

"I read a story once," I said, "called Jack and the

<104>

Beanstalk." I told him the story as I understood it, about how a boy named Jack got distracted on his way to town and traded his cow for magic beans. Who wouldn't? A cow will only nourish you as long as it's alive but magic beans will last forever, like all magic. When he planted the beans in his backyard, a giant tree popped up overnight.

"What kind of tree?" Bud asked.

"Why?" I replied, which he accepted as perfect sense, so I continued. "The tree grew all the way up into the clouds. If we could get beans like that, we'll grow a new tree right away. The tallest one around."

Bud thought about it for a long moment. Then he said, "We have no cow." Which in his dialect sounded like, "We have know how." So I was under the impression he approved. We stood there quietly, in complete agreement.

For months, Bud avoided that section of the estate, not wanting to rehash memories. This left fending for themselves all the wildlife that survived under the care of his great green thumb. They did not fare so well. It was to save their lives, as well as Bud's, that Bryan brought home the magic beans.

"What if," Bryan said, "you keep the roots in the ground, and carve a replica of your departed wife from the live stump? Then you plant it above her grave. As time goes by she'll grow up through the roots and inhabit the tree. Then you can be with her again."

<105>

I don't know how to describe the look on Bud's face, but I can say he modulated a full tone as he tried to make sense of this fantastical idea. His gardening experience dictated it was not possible, but his imagination dictated it was.

And so he set about carving the tree stump.

<106>

TWENTY-SIX

HOPES OF BRYAN having a real friend and my getting easy access to the roof increased manyfold when Connie invited him to her house for the weekend. Being teens, nearly, this idea required clearance from both sets of parents. Avarice was elated that Bryan had made a friend. Earnie didn't say anything. As a matter of fact, I hadn't seen him since that day on the sidewalk a few weeks earlier.

I admit I was a bit nervous about meeting Connie's parents. Foolish, but true nonetheless. If she were any indication, they'd be wonderful people. Then, of course, there was Miles. Maybe he was adopted.

Constants set the tone from the start, introducing him by name, Bryan, occupation, student, and place of residence, Long Island.

Any question we did not answer was quickly answered for us. They had an encyclopedia of polite reasons why he could not respond: he was tired, he was quiet, the train trip must have been long. They seemed to know more about him than I did. There was a lot of smiling and nodding.

Here, my phonetic friend, is where a most irksome art form need be mentioned. An art form so nebulous, it has no wall space in any museum, no section in any encyclopedia, or any curriculum in schools. An art form so fleeting, it can only be understood at the time of its inception, and then it's best to let it dissipate in the wind, like smoke signals. That art form is small talk.

What do you say when you have nothing to say?

Ironically, the best way to speak is to ask questions. Most people love to talk about themselves, and it keeps their inquisitiveness at bay. We weren't particularly worried, though. Bryan and I had been together long enough to establish a complete cover story, so it was no problem talking about ourself when necessary. Between the two of us, when we couldn't dazzle we'd baffle.

Connie's father, Mr. O'Really, was an agreeable person, a maintenance man at Carnegie Hall. He was totally committed to his family. Many people flail about in unbounded confusion looking for the next big thing, what stock will make them rich, what deal will set them free, what lottery ticket will hold the winning numbers. They search for the venue

<108>

that will bring them fame and fortune and, by extension, happiness. He had found his venue, right here at home. He made it look easy, but I know he worked hard every day to get to that place. Practice, practice, practice.

Like Avarice, he was an OctaVarian, but in a lower register, not at all offensive. He had complete control over his dynamics. He was a conductor, a maestro really, and this was his concert hall. So when he said, "You're Bernie and Alice's kid," I didn't question him. "You got quite a reputation. Off to college already."

"Actually, Daddy, he graduated college," Connie bragged. "He's going for a Master's."

"Really? Can you program my VCR? HA!" he laughed.

"You still use the analog format?" I asked, hoping it was true.

He looked confused. "Huh?"

"It's vastly superior. More reliable than digital. It's rusty plastic, you know? Old recording tape is nothing more than rust sprinkled on plastic."

"Really?" he said, barely concealing his puzzlement. About what, I'm not sure.

"We have Tivo," Connie quickly offered, followed just as quickly by her mother: "It's so easy, you don't even know you're using it." Then she said, half to herself, half aloud, "Where's the challenge in that?"

Mrs. O'Really was in transition. She was beginning

<109>

to think out loud, a pre-emptive empty-nest defense mechanism. It's nice to be able to wonder aloud. You can do that when you're at home with loved ones. Real loved ones.

If Mr. was a conductor, Mrs. was a composer, of all the good things Connie did, of all the maintenance Mr. did at Carnegie Hall, Mrs. O'Really scripted it all from here. The two of them collaborated on the most beatific opera I'd ever attended.

She had plenty to do outside of the family as well. She was the local confidante. Friends and neighbors trusted her with their secrets: confessions of deception, adultery, and substance abuse. An individual's secrets can get heavy, never mind those of an entire entourage, suburbanites trying to keep up with their favorite characters on TV, those whose lives seem to be so much more valuable. People care more about you when you're on TV than they do about themselves.

As everyone secreted their problems in her cupboard, Mrs. O'Really was running out of room. She stored them up like leftovers, sealed tight in Ziploc bags. For those with saucier scandals, she had Tupperware.

Because their secrets became hers from the listening, Mrs. O'Really needed an outlet. While friends received absolution through confession, she had nowhere to go for exoneration. She couldn't share their secrets without violating their trust, so wonder-

<110>

ing aloud became her pressure valve.

I think she could have shared with her husband. He was a good guy. I mean, he was no pastor, but I'm sure he wouldn't have spilled the beans.

She herself had no lies. Except for one: she had been diluting the morning coffee with decaf, out of concern for her husband's health.

What would she do if her husband left, too?

Plan ahead, Mama. The second half of your life is half as long as the first.

She spoke of getting a part-time job, but her inner dialogue was fraught with doubt. I can hear it now.

"What do you do?"

"Well, I make eggs."

"A short-order cook?"

"I conceive, gestate, and give birth. Then I breast-feed."

"A stripper?"

"I raised two children."

"A babysitter?"

"No."

"A maid?"

"No."

"A cow?"

"Certainly not."

"What exactly do you think you'll bring this company?"

"Together," should be her answer. But how do you put that on a resume?

<111>

I suggested she paste a series of family photographs, beginning with her wedding, then of first-born Miles, then add Constants, and so on. Each photograph would have a caption describing what a mother must do to create a family. The O'Really brochure. They all laughed at me.

"Where do I put my typing speed? Next to knitting?"

One couldn't help but love this woman, this household, and this family.

"What were you doing at Rockefeller Center there, Bryan?" Mr. O'Really inquired.

"I've always had a keen interest in television."

"You're a pretty good-lookin' guy. I could see you on TV. Right, hon?"

"Daddy, please," Connie implored.

"What?"

Then Mrs. O'Really said, "Well, we should sit down to supper."

If I heard her correctly, she said "supper" with two "p's". And all those years on the estate I thought they were "f's."

<112>

TWENTY-SEVEN

THROUGHOUT THE EVENING Miles continued his furtive assault on Bryan, always muttering, glaring suspiciously. What did he have to be so angry about? Look at this home, such a stable stable. A loving family, a wife to be, and an established sky diving business, all within fifteen kilometers. He left after dinner, off to his fiancée's.

I wonder if they'll get a dog?

I don't know if Miles was a devout hunter or a rabid garage sailor, but his bedroom had more dead animals in it than a pet cemetery. It was a taxidermist's trophy case, head upon head of the dead. Thankfully, there were no boobies or frigates, but I wondered if any of my old friends were hanging around. This is certainly how I'd end up if I were to be discovered.

It was quiet in there. Too quiet. I couldn't sleep, but for all the wrong reasons. I grabbed a blanket and retired to the back porch, where I hoped to catch some z's.

The air was muggy, but less so than in the city or on the island, the long one. Oddly enough, I found the sound of the crickets soothing. When I was a bat, I never would have settled for that racket. I'd have summoned my brethren and Luftwaffed every last one of those noisy insects to dreamland. Sure, we decimated entire populations, but I never knew a bat with an insignia on its wings.

I nodded off, the sleep of the innocent. There was time enough for a few pleasant dreams before I awakened, momentarily forgetting where I was or how far I'd traveled.

The grass fluttered, but not from the wind. The blades were bowing down, providing traction where they might otherwise be slippery. I heard toes gripping the lawn, and breaths rhythmic, deep, and regular. Her sharply defined figure glided across the horizon, its contours precise and exact. Maybe it was my imagination, or cunning adumbrations, but I swear the trees tilted towards her when she exhaled.

She stepped up onto the deck, soaking wet, a towel protecting her torso. The moonlight winked at me in the beads of water as they slid down her skin like shooting stars. I made a wish.

Her hair was perfectly slicked back, dark and drip-

<114>

ping, thick and clinging to her head, accentuating her perfectly shaped cranium. Even in this exposed state, she was a model of strength.

"Why are you out here? Isn't Mike's room comfortable?" she asked.

"Mike's," she'd said, with a "k" instead of an "l." She was only off by a single letter. I could work with that.

"I like the sounds of nature."

She lay on the next lounge chair, wrapping herself snug as a bug, but not before I scanned her for tattoos. None.

"Where were you?" I asked, somewhat envious that she'd been swimming.

"There's a pond a few houses down. Don't say anything. My parents would freak if they knew I did this."

"I won't. I love the water, too."

"I remember. I was there at Bay Hills pool that day you lost your suit. Dang, Brain, you acted like you lost your wallet down there," she said lightheartedly. "You really pitched a fit."

She'd started calling him "Brain" instead of Bryan, sort of a pet name. It was endearing.

Bryan chuckled, a little embarrassed. "I like the water. What can I say?"

"You're a water child. No doubt. What's your sign?"

"Slow, children at play."

<115>

"Ha!" she blurted out heartily. She got it on the first take! No instant replay. No explanation. The only person ever to do so with such regularity.

"You must be a Cancer," she continued. "What's your birthday?"

"Sometime in June. Seven or nine."

"What? First of all, no it isn't because you're not a Gemini. You're definitely a water sign. Probably Pisces. And second, seven or nine? Earth to Bryan. When did your mother pop you out? I think she'd remember. Was it the seventh or the ninth?"

He explained the vagaries of his birthday on the estate.

"They traveled a lot, so…"

"Uh huh," she said, unconvinced but willing to drop it without further ado. "Pisces. Two fish. And happy to be that way. Which might explain why you don't have any friends."

"I have friends."

"What, like online? Are you one of them? All your friends are out there in cyberspace?"

"Are you looking forward to going away?" I asked, quickly changing the subject, not wanting to explain his aversion to electronics.

"Sometimes. I'll miss my folks."

I missed mine, too.

"Let me ask you something," she said. "So that time on the monkey bars with Sheppard Davis. What did you say to him? You leaned into him and

<116>

said something that just," she glanced back into the house to see if anyone else could hear before she continued, "F'd him up. I mean, it was like you sucked his brain right out of his head. I think he wet his pants. What did you say to him?"

I was impressed she didn't want her parents to hear her mutter expletives, even if they were truncated.

Bryan told her what he said to Sheppard. She didn't get it at first.

"We were on the 'monkey' bars," he hinted.

A gigantic grin crossed her face. "Bloody hell. That's awesome." She was as impressed as I had been. "See. You're not so…" she trailed off. I got the feeling she was covering her tracks, trying to back-pedal. "Maybe someday I could read some of your stuff."

"I'll see what I can do. Most of it's up here," he said, tapping his temple.

"You don't have your writing, uh, written?"

"Some. Not much." Which was not entirely true. He wrote quite a bit, and I had been documenting as much as I could.

"I take it back. You are weird."

Which, I'm guessing, is what she stopped herself from saying moments before.

Eager to keep the conversation going, Bryan asked her why she chose an all-girls school.

"Like I want Buffy crying on my shoulder all night

<117>

cuz of something Skip said? Boys just add confusion. Not for me, I mean. I like them. I'm not saying I don't, but... It's not like I meet a lot of 'em anyway."

"Why not?"

"Look at me."

"I am."

"I'm not like most girls."

"Neither am I."

She laughed. "I'm not exactly the homecoming queen, you know?"

"I don't know what that means." But it was rife with possibilities.

"Queen of the Prom? Cheerleader? What do they teach you in home schooling?"

"How to stay at home."

"Hot? Sexy? Beautiful?"

"That is absurd. You're as beautiful as there is. You're nearly perfectly symmetrical." By the look on her face, I should have stopped right there. "Well-developed musculature. A slightly protruding frontal lobe. Well-shaped cranium. Robust hair follicles."

"Did you just say robust?"

"Your hair is very healthy, indicating..."

"I'll have to remember that one. Robust."

"Robust: strong and healthy," I quoted straight from the dictionary.

"Fat!"

She was stocky. Her arms and legs were thicker than Bryan's, but it was all muscle as far as I could see.

"Do you think you're fat?"

"Other people do."

"And that's where you should go. Where other people think healthy girls are better candidates for breeding. Places where people think you're more desirable."

"Keep digging, Brain. You may find that world."

"If you don't fit in where you are, go someplace else, someplace where you do. It's not rocket science."

"Uh huh."

"You know, the farther you go from Earth, the lighter you become."

"Great. I've always wanted to live on a cloud. Bring my family and friends. We could start a colony. What would we call it?"

"FrenZupon."

"Friends Upon. Sounds perfect. Connie O'Reilly…"

I'd like to buy a vowel.

"…Queen of the Friends Upon Prom. And you, you'll be, you know, normal."

"Reality is perception," I said.

"Maybe in our new world," she replied. "But in this world I'm robust, and robust doesn't make me easy on the eyes."

"Well, you're easy on the ears."

"Ears. Yeah. That's what you are, Brain. Eerie. You're one eerie dude."

She seemed to have put my inadvertent affront

<119>

aside, relaxing back into the lounge chair and putting her hands behind her head, dreamily.

"Tell me a story," she said. "I need something to get my mind off of going away."

I feared I might have said too much already, so I went silent, passing the torch to Bryan, though I stayed close at hand in case of emergency.

Poetry was Bryan's first love, but he went with prose this time and, as always, he did not disappoint.

It went something like:

"Simon used to sit in the sun room, watching the seasons change on the outside wall of the garage. As autumn's shadows swept in, naked branches with clinging leaves left blueprints to worlds far beyond the wall. One windy October 13th, there unfolded a most delightful rendering of stick figures from a shady rural village at a square dance. They were quite a flexible populace. Their limbs bent and rebounded with amazing agility as they danced the days away.

"Later in the year, as the sun shifted and the wind slowed, everyone gathered for Bingo at the community center. The town was not very affluent, so prizes consisted of free rides on a fire truck and a state lottery ticket. That Christmas Mrs. Slaterprice donated a beautiful hand-knit sweater she had been working on all year long for her husband. She had no more use for it as her husband had died earlier in December, frozen to death while ice fishing. In a strange

<120>

twist of fate, young Laurie Ingles won the sweater. It was much too large for her so she gave it to her father, Mr. Ingles.

"The following Easter Mrs. Ingles died tragically at the town picnic. She fell during the three-legged race and hit her head while attached to her husband. Doctor Sawyer said if she had been wearing her bonnet, it would have cushioned the blow and perhaps saved her life.

"Seven months later, the widow Slaterprice married the widower Ingles, so her husband did in fact wear the sweater she knitted. The wedding took place on the side of the garage, November 10th. Father McGuiness presided. Simon says, the end."

"You just make that up?"

"Yep."

"Damn, Brain. You are good."

That was all Bryan. I didn't add a single word. It was the first time we ever shared a story of his with anyone else. I thought it went quite well. I liked his style. It was similar to mine.

They looked at each other and smiled.

You're probably expecting sex here, my fornicating friend. But there won't be any. Which is not to say Bryan wasn't interested. He was at an age when the urges were emerging. But Connie didn't seem to be leading him there, and neither was I. I had never participated in a mating ritual and I wasn't about to start now.

< 1 2 1 >

TWENTY-EIGHT

BOARDING THE TRAIN for the city the next day, I felt rejuvenated. It seemed easier to focus on the immediate, to distinguish between those conversations we could actually see as well as hear.

I felt welcomed by the O'Reallys, like I belonged. If all else failed, if Bryan was expatriated before you came to my rescue, perhaps they would adopt me. With her flock flying the coop, Mrs. O'Really needed someone to fill her empty nest. That would mean Miles and I would be brothers. We should get to know each other better. On some breezy afternoon, I'd stop by his place of work and we'd go skydiving. As we fell to earth, we'd chat. He might even let me use his old bedroom, and I'd be happy to sleep there, assuming he didn't leave his heads behind.

Of course, I'd have to learn their oblique language.

It was like they shuffled letters, added and subtracted here and there. I'd figure it out. I figured out Bud's partial parlance. When I was just a pup I read entire books without knowing the language in which they were written. The O'Reallys weren't that far off. Actually, their version of reality was the closest to mine that I'd ever found. There was some sort of connect... connec...

A connection had come loose. Bursts of static interference short-circuited our thoughts. There was snow on the screen, dry leaves crackling on the track. An internal alarm sounded. My head popped up. My ears went back. I began panting, distressed. I scanned our vitals. But for the increased heart rate, all was normal. We were not in physical danger, but we were experiencing a programming error, instructions from long ago, another lifetime.

The crackling was the sound of a newspaper bunched in the left hand, flipping through pages with the right. I'd know that sound anywhere. It was those soft, unused hands. Of course he was at the back of the newspaper. That's where his ilk went to study the television listings.

As the train slowed, the conductor announced the station stop over the very loudspeaker. I heard the newspaper crumple and drop on the seat. The ninety-nine-cent sandals slithered out the door.

We snuck after him.

There'd be no going home today. This train was taking us to a very different past.

< 123 >

TWENTY-NINE

HE WENT THROUGH the parking lot and across the street, stopping at a deli to pick up beer. About a block and a half later he walked into a dilapidated house with moldy vinyl siding and a screen door mounted on misaligned hinges, one of which was not even fully secured to the frame. The pneumatic door closer had no gas and a chain hung loosely from one end, serving no purpose whatsoever, much like the occupant.

We stayed back, across the street, keeping a watchful eye. I was beside myself, unsure of what to do. Part of me wanted to bolt, but the other part had other ideas.

We should come back when he's not here. We should tie him to a stake like a dog. What of Sous? Is she still here, or did she move on? If so, peaceably and intact, or did she wing it like I did?

I needed answers.

I walked onto the front porch and reached for the screen door. Its cheap aluminum frame was so oxidized it felt like sandpaper. It squeaked loudly. We hesitated briefly, then Bryan stuck his head into the kitchen. There on the counter, a plastic fan roiled the acrid air, making the flies work overtime in their struggle toward the oil stain at the center of a weeks-old pizza box.

He tortured even the flies.

The fan couldn't clear the stench, but its noise served as cover. We twinkle-toed through the kitchen into the living room.

There he was, sitting, drinking, watching TV. Hennessy. He had not moved up in the world, and as up was the only direction he had to go, he hadn't moved at all. The recliner he loved was gone, probably pawned for beer money. You can take the man out of the La-Z-Boy, but you can't take the La-Z-Boy out of the man.

The room was a grungy trash heap. Sous had been the primary housekeeper. Clearly, she was long gone. There was no indication whatsoever of a puppy, nor a family life of any kind, no souvenirs, mementos, photographs on the mantelpiece, which I now saw was faux brick.

Maybe Hennessy had erased me. Maybe he had a special power that allowed him to obliterate his

<125>

memories, to select pieces of his partial existence and snap them together in hopes it would add up to a life worthwhile. He was that special kind of idiot who needed an Exacto knife to do a jigsaw puzzle.

I had no such power. My memories of him were carved in granite and I shouldered them everywhere, from his house to the greenhouse to the white house to the bottom of the pool. If I could hate him as a sweet, innocent puppy, you can imagine how the rage swelled in the body of a young man.

We walked up behind him, within arm's reach.

The television screen went to black, between commercials. There was Bryan in the reflection, as clear as a reality star. Hennessy didn't see him. He was too lazy, staring blankly at the blank screen.

I'd forgotten how tall Bryan had grown, almost unmanageably so. Where had I been these last few years? I hardly recognized him. Right under my nose, his childish features had evolved into young adulthood. He looked good. It got me thinking we should include video in our distress message. It was a bit late now, but if this attempt failed, we'd use it in the next iteration. It adds a certain gravitas.

Poof. The reflection vaporized, replaced by more mind-numbing material for Hennessy's consumption.

That's when I saw it. Crippled beneath the weight of the television, at the bottom of the flotsam, camouflaged beneath the piles of rubbish, my old sanc-

<126>

tuary, my submarine, my spaceship. The sideboard. The place where everything was hunky-dory. It was un-serviced, chipped and haggard, like it had been transported by inept movers who held it for ransom until the balance was paid.

Memories washed over me.

"Ohm. Ohm. A G and C."

Hennessy jumped out of his chair, the quickest I'd ever seen him move.

"Hey! Who the hell are you?" he yelled, his voice cracking, his eyes bulging. He was coiled, ready to pounce, or run.

Bryan assumed no such posture. Neither Bryan nor I felt threatened by him, so we just continued to stare.

I smelled fear.

Bryan was intimidating. After seeing his reflection, I could understand how sometimes people were afraid of him. But most of the time people never were. Usually.

"Get the hell outta here!" Hennessy yelled.

Bryan stayed steely. I laughed, confident in my new stature. What will you do, Hennessy? Will you pick on someone your own size and species? Or be a fraidy-cat and run into the bathroom and lock the door?

He ran into the bathroom and locked the door.

"I've got a gun, you son of a…" his voice disintegrated into a whimper.

<127>

He probably didn't have a gun. I mean, who keeps a gun in the toilet? That's stupid, even for him.

We assessed Hennessy's threat level to be near zero, so we took the opportunity to explore the sideboard. Bryan was as anxious as I to see what treasures awaited. The doors were jammed. We rabidly tried to open them, tugging, pulling, prying…

No!

One swift bludgeon from the steel toe of Bryan's work boot, and the wooden door splintered to pieces. Another sanctuary gone. People take things away on a whim, just to satisfy their own immediate needs.

We shuffled through the clutter, looking for a collar, a tennis ball, a squeaky toy. But there was nothing. Not even a pee mail. It was as if I'd never existed, that my time in this house never happened.

Just as sad, now I understood what I had been reading all the time I was sequestered in here. The magazines, the maps, the textbooks and travelogues, the brochure for Scuba, they were all pieces of Sous, her unwritten diary, her secreted hopes, things she did not do, places she did not go, topics she did not study. Dreams destroyed by insomnia, Ambien, and ambivalence, courtesy of the ape locked in the bathroom, captain of the cruise ship *Apathy*. Destination procrastination.

Life is like traveling, isn't it? You can read the brochures, look at the pictures, find places on a map, but you don't really know what it's like until you get

<128>

there.

Sous was a star, one of the highlights of my lives. I didn't suppose Hennessy would tell me where to find her, so I could only hope she had moved on to greener pastures.

"I called the cops!" I'm pretty sure I heard.

We'd rummaged long enough. This was just going to end in trouble. Bryan grabbed a few things and stuffed them into his pocket.

In the corner of my eye I saw a photograph, tucked in a crack between the bottom and back of the drawer. It was one I'd never seen. A portrait. A family portrait. The two of them, Mr. and Mrs. Hennessy, with plastic smiles painted on their faces, and a child, an infant. His eyes were wide, buggy, and his smile was crooked, sort of cranked open. It looked like a ventriloquy doll whose operator suffered a ruptured aneurism in the middle of a punch line and dropped his alter ego on its head, knocking a few screws loose and locking its jaw in the middle of a guffaw.

It was most disturbing. I felt another urge in Bryan beginning to bubble. Something about seeing that little boy with his black as onyx eyes and nightmare hair, gazing blindly off into never-never land, made him angry. He wanted to kick down the bathroom door, get his hands on Hennessy's skinny neck, and grind his bones to make his bread.

"Ohm. Ohm. A G and C."

<129>

Storming out of the bathroom, Hennessy was upon us instantly, landing a solid punch straight to Bryan's jaw. He had a roll of pennies clenched in his fist that supplemented the impact. It seemed like a waste of good lunch money, and it only worked once.

The roll of coins burst out of his hand, a puking piggy bank, a washed-up wishing well spitting back every lost hope ever tossed into its scummy puddle, returning the unfulfilled dreams, denied for insufficient postage.

Bryan fell to the floor, dazed. Fortunately, I was accustomed to working without a body and I knew Hennessy's tactics. He jumped on top of us and managed to land a few more blows, but they were ineffectual. Those soft, unused hands didn't pack the wallop they did when I was a puppy, especially without his copper supplements.

He had broken me before, but I wasn't going to let that happen again. Not to me. Not to Bryan. Not this time.

I reached up with one hand and easily brushed him aside, wrestled him to the ground, and held him immobile. He was squirming like a worm sliding onto a fishing hook. I was careful not to throw any punches. I wanted him to be cognizant, awake and aware, to look into Bryan's eyes and see me, the puppy he destroyed.

I didn't know what I was going to say. I couldn't rightly bark at him. That'd be just plain weird. But

<130>

he should know who had come to pay respects, to collect a bill long past due.

Bryan came up with the perfect words, naturally. He leaned close to Hennessy, so close he could singe him with his burning, black eyes, and delivered a dish of arctic acrimony.

"Every dog has his day."

He should be writing greeting cards, right?

Hennessy's breaths became short and shallow. Did I mention we were squeezing his neck? The look on his face was going from blank to blanker as the few functioning brain cells went fleeing for their lives.

With those refugees went Hennessy's meager cognitive ability. As such, the violence became fruitless. No matter what I said or how hard we squeezed, he was not going to see me. He would never understand who I was or why this was happening. He had wiped his slate clean long ago.

I loosened my grip. But Bryan compensated, squeezing harder.

I implored him to desist. If this becomes a crime scene and we are taken into custody, I'll be stuck for who knows how much longer. A police psychologist could be more electrifying than Doctor Chris.

Who would know?

There'd be fingerprints.

Maybe not. Remember the razor blades? They probably made any fingertip identification impossible.

< 1 3 1 >

200 hertz!

But violence is only acceptable as self-defense.

250 hertz!

We were attacked.

300 hertz!

Hennessy is neutralized.

350 hertz!

"Ohm. Ohm. A G and C."

Wait a minute. Did I see that correctly? The brochure for Scuba? It's not a tropical destination at all. It's an activity! You know, you learn something new every day, or two.

What was I just saying?

Oh, yes. Strangling Hennessy.

Dear old dud appeared blue, a deep blue, like mood indigo. I released my grip on his throat. I wouldn't say I forgave him, so much as I pardoned him.

I don't know what Bryan did.

<132>

THIRTY

BRYAN'S ADRENAL GLANDS were in overdrive. We walked, for hours, through the small hamlet of wherever the train stopped. Suffern, I suppose.

Maybe we could take a train to Orange? I've always wanted to live in Orange.

We passed by seemingly friendly people, many of whom nodded most graciously. As kindly as they acted, I knew the absolute truth: given the proper circumstances, they would do exactly what I did. Never mind the bucolic setting, the scent of the bakery or the fragrance of freshly cut grass. If all that fell apart, if chocolate were poisonous, if we pried every smiling mouth open just a little wider, there would be fangs, just like every other animal.

We continued our trek through town. After about a kilometer and a half, we veered off the road. The sounds of lawn mowers and shredders faded away. We stopped in a clearing at the top of a long ridge. The view was forever. The sun was sinking below the horizon, setting the world ablaze in transcendent colors.

"HEY!" Bryan yelled, but his voice was stolen by the wind.

"HEY!" I yelled. But there was nobody here, so there was nothing to hear.

I considered returning to Connie's, but we'd passed the point of no return. The trail of breadcrumbs I dropped on my way has been eaten by hungry birds, my footprints in the sand long since taken by the tide.

<134>

THIRTY-ONE

WAS IT MILES who suggested we visit the zoo? I think so. I can't remember. It's a most offensive place, much more so than the museum. Mercifully, Miles didn't come inside with us. He waited in the café. And it was a good thing, too. One look at the cages full of prix fixe prey and he'd be off with their heads.

Connie was miffed when she saw Bryan's black eye. He explained it away as an accident he suffered helping Bud in the yard. It was an ugly bruise. No matter the excuse, it looked violent.

Perhaps I should have waited a few days until the black eye healed, but Connie was leaving soon. Bryan was leaving soon. And hopefully, I was leaving soon. The summer was coming to a close. School buses were already clogging the main arteries. Time was evanescent.

It's funny that way, time. The more you take, the less you have.

Bryan and I had become unwound since the altercation with Warden, unglued really. Looking at that little boy in the photo felt like bathing in turpentine. It stripped the whitewash from the picket fence of the Norman Roswell portrait we had been living in.

It wasn't necessarily a biological child. It could have been adopted, probably after I left. That's what many young couples do. They practice on a puppy, then graduate to the real thing. If Hennessy had reproduced, though, and spread those noxious genes, it would be a tragedy. Nature-nurture aside, his DNA is a four-letter word.

For all our polite conversation, Connie's demeanor was guarded, as was the tenor of her voice. She was trying to keep it at an even decibel as if to soothe Bryan's mind or heal his eye. She inquired, ever so gingerly, about his return trip to the city. Was the train ride long? Did he make it home OK?

She was keeping the chatter bland and generic, and I had the distinct impression she did not want to be there.

"I got my first housing choice," Connie shared, referring to dormitory room assignments.

I was glad about that. Leaving home was not easy for her, so the little things were big. I was excited she'd brought up housing. It provided a perfect segue to the idea of Bryan living with her family.

<136>

"That's great," I replied. "The home you have now is very nice, too."

"Thanks."

"Very comfortable."

"Thanks."

"Your parents are nice, too."

"Thanks."

She was awfully thankful, but wasn't taking the bait.

We meandered through the zoo, as well as topics of conversation. With each display we passed and each topic we covered, things became more awkward. I couldn't help but think it had to do with Bryan's battle scar.

We arrived at the polar bear den. That's a genus I never inhabited, too olfactory for my tastes. But I would have gladly traded places with them at that moment. The water looked so cool and inviting, and it had been a long time since Bryan and I had had an in-depth conversation.

The heat was disorienting. Bryan's eye was throbbing, his skin crawling as though every hair on his adolescent body was attached to a nine-volt battery.

At least it was a paltry nine volts.

"Do you know this guy had therapy?" Connie mused.

I listened closely for clarification. She was indeed referring to the polar bear.

"It's true," she continued. "Years ago one of the

<137>

bears swam around in circles, so they brought in a bear psychologist to figure out why."

How perfect is that? Call a shrink to ask a polar bear why he doesn't like being taken from the vast expanse of the tundra and crammed into a fifty-foot pen in the middle of a city. They should be asking the people who absconded with the poor bastard why they felt the need to steal him in the first place.

"I mean he just swam around and around," she continued. "It's kinda weird, you know?"

"What? The bear swimming around, or that they thought he needed therapy?"

"Huh?" she muttered, obviously not in sync with us.

"Maybe the bear got scared when he saw the penguins next door. He was trying to swim back to the Arctic because he thought he was on the wrong side of the world."

"Cute," she said. "But I don't think they're that aware."

"That's the problem. Nobody thinks he's aware, but he is. He knows he doesn't belong here. So he's disassociating himself from his surroundings. A zoo is an abnormal place and he's trying to compensate."

"Bryan." She looked at him with concern.

"Why is it the ones who don't accept abnormal are abnormal?"

"Are you OK?" she said, with that deliberate pitch.

"Why don't they return him home instead of try-

<138>

ing to cram him in with the penguins?"

"You know, Bryan," Connie said anxiously, "I think we ought to go find my brother."

"Why do you keep swimming around in circles?" I continued, mimicking the many shrinks we'd endured. I could hear my volume increasing, but I was powerless to govern it. "The next thing you know, they'll be interrogating you to see why you began menstruating before the legal age of eighteen!"

She stood there agape, then hoofed it toward the exit. I followed, trying to explain, but I couldn't blurt anything intelligible. Bryan was restricting access to his mouth, trying to subdue the developing spectacle. "Don't make a scene, what happens when you start to wonder aloud? Everyone heads for the exits! A G and see no evil. Don't hear or speak, either. Not out loud!"

She quickened her pace.

Our own commotion was drowned out by another of greater size. It was feeding time at the sea lion tank. A large group of mostly tourists and partly patrons gathered to watch something else eat. There was quite a stir as a trainer issued forth with a bucket of fish. I lost Connie in the crowd as I found myself caught up in the alimentary distraction at center stage.

The water in the tank was swirling, bubbling from the gathering of ravenous abdomens. It was impossible to tell how many prisoners were inside. I hoped

<139>

for the animals' sake no more than two. I was wrong. I counted at least four as they leapt up onto the rocks to greet their waiter. They shook hands and did stands, and were promptly rewarded with fish and applause.

Then I saw Mimi, a friend of a friend I'd known from my time as a sea anemone. She jumped up onto a rock and kissed the feeder right on the lips. She'd had a reputation, but I never thought she'd stoop to such levels, doing kisses and flips for her fish and chips. I wouldn't have believed it if I didn't see it myself.

I needed a better vantage point, so I sprang up onto the edge of the containment tank.

"Mimi!"

She craned her neck and we momentarily caught eyes.

"Mimi, it's me!"

She quickly looked back at the trainer, pretending not to notice me.

With no help from Bryan, I tried to walk toward her, but he allowed me only two left feet.

What was I thinking? What was I doing? I don't even know. Was I going to rescue her from that madhouse before they drove her crazy, like they did the polar bear?

I lost my balance and fell in. The water was cool and awakening, and snapped me out of whatever state I'd sunken into. I clawed my way out of the sea lion brine and exited the zoo before security arrived.

< 140 >

THIRTY-TWO

MIMI IGNORED ME for good reason. Had she acknowledged me, zoo officials would've associated her with the nut causing the disturbance and returned her to the wild, replacing her with someone less splashy.

Or maybe she had completely forgotten who she was in her earlier life. I was worried that was happening to me. I wanted to be able to report everything exactly as it happened. But who knows? After Hennessy's, I was more confused than ever. I mean, look at how wrong I was about Scuba! Little things like that made me question myself. And that's never a good thing, because if you don't give yourself the right answer, you're in serious trouble.

Apologies to Connie's smart phone went unanswered as well. Miles was probably censoring her calls. I could hear him now. Not literally, just imaginarily. "I told you this guy is no good. You wanna jeopardize your scholarship? You shouldn't hang out with him. He's not safe."

Not safe? Doesn't he know I pardoned someone the other day, saved somebody's life, a life that deserved to end?

The outburst at the zoo was a strike against us, certainly more than most people would tolerate. But Connie was special. She knew Bryan, and liked him for his differences. And we liked her for the same reasons.

It was time I leveled with her. If I explained what was really going on with me and Bryan, she'd understand. She'd probably even offer help.

I'd meet her next Tuesday at the blood bank.

THIRTY-THREE

I WAITED FOR her outside, too afraid to go in. I had this nagging feeling that if I entered, they'd force me to donate a lifetime supply. Why not? There are no boundaries with them. If they smell the blood of an english muffin, they'll take it. And I wasn't feeling particularly poriferous, or groovy.

The old brown air conditioner looked worse on the outside than in, and was much louder. The sidewalk beneath it was stained red from the rusty water leaking out of its depressed compressor. Two pieces of wood were wedged beneath it, holding it in place. Over time, the vibrations had carved a notch in the wood and in that notch, the frame rested snugly. It was the vibrating that kept this old contraption in place. If they ever pulled the plug and the chassis stopped rattling, it would fall out of the window and shatter on the concrete.

It had a good buzz going, so I hopped on and rode shotgun while we waited for reinforcements.

When I was a molecule of fibrinogen, I participated in some kind of blood-clotting test. It was more like a fire drill, lots of sirens and beeping and screaming. For all our training, we were not able to clot. We bandied about, trying to agree upon a direction, but could not reach consensus.

Once we realized our efforts were futile, that we could not stop the hemorrhaging and we no longer had purpose, all sense of order disintegrated. It became every cell for itself. We stampeded through the epidermis like buffalo over amber waves of grain. I knew we wouldn't survive outside. We weren't cut out for it. I tried to restore order, to stem the mass exodus, but I got caught up in the rush. If we had stuck together, we could have saved our hostess and ourselves. Instead, she died, and soon enough the same would happen to us. I wasn't about to become a stigmartyr.

So I left.

<144>

THIRTY-FOUR

"WHAT THE HELL are you doing here?"

Miles stood there looking as Paleolithic as ever. I didn't even hear him approaching. That's how out of tune I was. Naturally I didn't say anything, because the answer should have been obvious.

"Let's get this clear right now," he continued. He must have seen my eyes wander because he snapped his fingers in front of my face. "Over here. Hey! Retard. Connie is not your friend. OK? She's not gonna hang out with you or have you over for dinner or anything. And if I ever see you hangin' out in our neighborhood, I'm gonna make sure you end up in jail or in the hospital. OK? She was nice to you cuz she felt sorry for you. I don't. You're a rich, spoiled little retard. So find someplace else to screw off to. Do you hear me? Do you hear me?"

I nodded yes, and Miles quickly departed.

Bryan's heart fell into his stomach. Or maybe it was mine.

I wasn't expecting this much pain. We both liked her, but I didn't realize just how much until that moment. It had been a long time since I'd had a broken heart. I don't think Bryan had ever had one, not since I'd been there. I wouldn't allow it. But this was my doing. I walked him right into it. I thought I was building a safety net and instead I weaved a web.

Constants was an un-popped kernel. We were cut from the same cloth. But like I said, never assume others are like you. She was cashmere and I was mohair. Just because we were cut from the same cloth didn't mean we were shorn from the same goat.

They tried to kill me with beatings, education, therapy, and drugs. But killing me with kindness was the most inhumane plot of all.

Now I know how Pluto felt.

I had to rethink my plan with a new parameter: Constants was no longer a variable.

<146>

THIRTY-FIVE

"Mother," I said to Avarice, back on the estate, "I've been thinking about a party. To celebrate my going away to the university."

Her smile cracked through her makeup, releasing a flood of relief. It had been a long time since I'd seen her smile.

"Oh, sweetie, that would be fabulous. It would be so very lovely to do something nice like that."

"I'd like it at The Rainbow Room." Which is way up in the Thir-D Rock Plaza.

"Oh," she said, not expecting such specificity. "Well, let's see what we can do. A celebration would be good. We'll invite everybody."

I didn't know who all everybody was, nor did I care. It would get us close to the roof of the broadcast facility and that's all I needed. A crowd would provide cover. It's easier to disappear with lots of people around. I was at a bit of a disadvantage without a tour guide or any sort of recon mission, but between the two of us I had no doubt we could pull it off. It was such a simple plan.

Theoretically.

<148>

THIRTY-SIX

IN THE OLD days, those divine days when insanity was profound, if a slave had the opportunity to go free and refused to do so, they would put out his ears with an awl.

Bryan and I were not slaves. We'd depended upon each other for a long time, but we agreed that time was coming to an end. Keeping me hidden had become a burden greater than he should bear. Look at what I did with Constants. I completely alienated her. Bryan tried to keep me in check that day at the zoo, but I lost focus. I couldn't predict his future, and I didn't want to influence it any longer.

The broadcasting center was my last best chance at survival, but from the recent visit it was obvious my resistance training had lost its vigor. Ohms and notes would not protect us, and we had no other tools to deal with the bile in the belly of the beast. We needed to neutralize our receptors. It was the only way to be sure the noise would not overwhelm us. Remember what Crosson said? Better to be deaf. It makes things so much simpler. And you can't argue with a guy who lived in a state of perpetual REM.

We went to the nursery in search of the specialized tool. There was the usual array of gardening and horticultural supplies: fertilizers, herbicides, pesticides, and other flavor-enhancing chemicals. But no awl. Nor was there any sign of Bud.

We found our way to the hole in the sky, where the tree had once stood, where now was a shed that Bud built around its stump. I could hear him inside. He was oscillating. We knocked on the door. He didn't respond, so we entered.

The man of earth sat on a shaky, three-legged stool, unshaved and unwashed, his hair matted with dirt and oil. His shirt had fled in search of cooler climes. His feet were buried in a pile of sawdust, like he was sprouting from the ground himself.

There was no carving. No statue. Just dust. He was crying.

In a mixture of languages only I could understand, he explained how he had chiseled the tree down, whittling away for months. While he had formed a lovely, supple smile, the eyes he'd fashioned always held a grain of sadness. He wanted to give it symmetry, perfection, to match the memories of his wife.

<150>

So notch by notch he chipped away, sheet by sheet he sanded. Until he carved but dust and space, alone and empty handed.

Now he blamed himself twice for her death, and from the looks of it, he planned to bury himself here with her.

Love and loss had sentenced Bud to isolation in this little shed. They'll do that, remove you from the rest of the world, strip you of your personality, and lock you in a sensory deprivation tank. All the addictions, treatments, parlor games, coliseums, deities, distractions, and affirmations one can develop will never change that. They're as sure as gravity, the laws of love and loss. Even one as grounded as Bud could be razed by them.

I thought the carving had a sort of parallel harmony. Why? Because often within one and the same person there is an imbalance: the mouth says one thing while the ears are hearing something else entirely. Even if everyone were prepared according to a recipe, we wouldn't always come out like the magazine photos. The slightest deviations in ingredients, altitude, oven temperature, or whisking method, and we could rise too high, fall too soon, or spill out of the mold completely. But that doesn't mean we should be taken off the menu, or even discounted.

It takes someone special, more special than Bud or I, to accept the terms of this paradox.

"Bud," Bryan said, "it is perfect. Your wife is dead.

<151>

I'm so sorry, my friend. As all things must, she's returned to dust. Our most beloved tree, the tallest, strongest one we knew, sacrificed itself in her honor. It put itself in your hands, with hopes that your wife could be properly represented. And you created a pile of dust. So you see, it is, in fact, a perfect replica of her. You should make topsoil. Spread it in the garden and see what grows."

Bud looked around at the dust as if it would translate. I guess it did, because his demeanor did a pirouette, and the weight of the earth was lifted from his heels.

<152>

THIRTY-SEVEN

WE CAME AWAY from the shed without an awl. But we had an alternative, the good old razor blade. No, we weren't going to go van Gogh. But with a Q-Tip and some crackerjack carving, we fashioned all the awl we needed.

We slid the sharpened Q-Tip into his right ear canal and poked around, looking for the drum. We found it and shoved it in! It was quick. And painful.

His eyes watered, but he didn't make a sound. Blood began to trickle from the puncture wound. I had that old feeling of fluid in the ear, but it also sounded like half the voices in the world were silenced, which was exactly what we wanted.

"Bryan."

I know it hurts, but we're halfway home.

"Bryan."

Avarice was standing in the doorway, looking at him in the bathroom mirror.

"What are you doing?" she said, at fifty percent volume.

Bryan turned away to hide his bleeding ear. "I think I have an ear infection."

"Have you been swimming?"

"Nope."

"Do you want me to put in ear drops?"

"No. I can do it."

"You have enough?"

"No, Mom. I'll be all right."

She struggled with her next words, her lung capacity shrunken from nervousness. Or maybe they were still full of denial and she couldn't empty them just yet.

"You know your father's not coming home."

We already knew. He had left with the woman he secretly met that day at the Chelsea Hotel.

"Yeah. I know."

I was never sure if Earnie felt anything, sad, angry, empty, or fulfilled. In the insulated playground of estate row, he was deeply hidden in the money pit. He just floated around on a magic carpet, buoyed by boundless bounty. He could afford to give Avarice half and half again. I didn't mind that he was gone, and I'm sure he didn't care that Bryan was leaving.

Avarice grabbed Bryan and hugged him tightly. She was trembling. I don't think she'd eaten a prop-

<154>

er meal since I knew her. She'd withered down to as much of an empty shell as my family of dead turtles.

I couldn't imagine her being the heroine in a story I once heard. The tour guide told it, during that phone call in Earnie's office years ago. It was the story of the delivery of a child, a human child, not a turtle.

As I remember it: the child's head was caught in his mother's womb, his posterior crowning first, his ass his ambassador. For quite some time his butt stuck out while the rest of his fussy little fetus clung to its embryonic heritage, all the while, mind you, being deprived of oxygen. If this had indeed been Bryan, it might explain where he learned to hold his breath for so long.

The doctor took emergency measures, declaring tug-of-war. He reached in and grasped whatever he could find. It was a hand. He pulled, dislocating its shoulder. Then a foot popped out so he pulled on that, and probably displaced its hip as well. The baby fought valiantly, but bit by bit he was pulled from his home. Popping out, he went airborne, the flight of the bumbling M.D. He landed on the floor, twisted in a position only a circus performer could attain, his slimy little limbs wrapped forwards and back. Most newborns receive a swat on their fannies to welcome them to the world. This poor kid was being drawn and quartered. Could a tar-and-feathering be far behind? If this was what the new world

<155>

had in store, he'd just as soon stay in the old one, thank you very much.

As a result of the destructive delivery, the mother was hemorrhaging uncontrollably, and…

That was all I heard. I didn't stick around for the ending. I made tracks to the greenhouse and the razor blade.

I could imagine Bryan surviving this ordeal. To be frank, it would explain some of his physical anomalies and his uniqueness of mind. But it doesn't jibe that Avarice was on the delivering end. She couldn't have been. She hadn't the fortitude or the physique to live through such an ordeal.

"I'm so proud of you," Avarice said, as she released Bryan and composed herself. The blood from Bryan's ear mixed with her tears and smudged her cheek. If she noticed, there's no telling how long we'd go away for.

She pulled a tissue, wiped her face, and discarded it in the wastebasket. The tissue, that is. She kept her face.

"Thanks, Ma."

She left.

We shut the door and proceeded.

<156>

THIRTY-EIGHT

"DON'T STOP. DON'T stop," we mumbled the entire elevator ride up to the Rainbow Room. If only it would keep going, blast through the roof and break through the atmosphere, the stratosphere, the ecosphere, and every other sphere, and on and on.

The dinner was attended by everyone who was anyone and no one I knew, dozens and dozens of thrice-removed cousins. They came by the droves, from estate row and who knows, and so many high-class locales.

They were polite, charming, and endearingly quiet. The women were all dressed uniquely; their outfits had nothing in common. If they were a hand of cards, I'd have to fold. The men were all dressed identically, jacket, slacks, and ties. If they were a hand of cards, I'd have a flush.

Avarice's family was there, too, her mom and dad. She had family? I'll be a monkey's uncle. And there was me, the uninvited guest, the party crasher, the one who just showed up.

I knew what everyone was saying, even though we couldn't hear them. It was a penthouse full of Mr. and Mrs. Marcel Marceaus.

I scanned the room thoroughly, noting the layout, paying careful attention to where the waitstaff entered and exited. That's where the service area would be and, most likely, an elevator or staircase to the roof. Fortunately, the party was crowded. Plenty of alcohol was being consumed and platitudes spewed. At any moment I'd sneak away. I was feeling hopeful.

But like I said, theories are always clear on paper. Then you take them into the battlefield and the fog of war descends.

Suddenly there was tidal shift in the room. Everyone turned almost simultaneously to face me, and something was springing from their lips. It looked like speech, speech.

They cleared a path, and we worked our legs until we came to be standing on a riser with a microphone in our face. All attention was focused on Bryan, and it was really, really quiet.

Is that all it takes to quiet people? Get a microphone and be louder? Like that guy on the sidewalk? Maybe then, as Mr. O'Really suggested, broadcast-

<158>

ing would be the ideal profession for Bryan.

I remembered how annoying it was when we were looked at, observed, and studied. But now, as the droves that drove me mad stood and stared, they were as quiet as mice and perfectly tolerable. It was one of the most satisfying moments I'd ever experienced. We all just looked at each other. Nobody said a word. I'm sure there were chairs creaking, throats clearing, and pins dropping, but I couldn't hear them.

My mouth got very dry. I tried to manufacture some saliva. I guess the jaw motion indicated impending words, because everyone redoubled their patiently waiting.

Don't worry. We knew this would happen, and Bryan had prepared a few words. It wasn't anything special, just a sweet, short "so long," completely innocent and disingenuous, but enough to keep red flags lowered.

He pulled a crumpled piece of paper out of his pocket. It felt a little different than the one we'd made notes on. It looked different, too, more crumpled than it should have been.

We had grabbed the wrong piece of paper. These were not the notes he made. This was not his adieu. But I didn't know just how very wrong a piece of paper it was until I unfolded it.

To the untrained eye it was nothing but chaotic cuneiform. It looked like an uneducated puppy had

<159>

scratched something out with its left paw.

he hades ere ide pen, itchen lean.
cy, arooma ashin ine.

It was the paper we took from the sideboard. On it was the poem Bryan wrote about my incarceration at Hennessy's.

But…

The world began to shake. I think a low-flying jet passed by, or maybe a helicopter was hovering just outside, somewhere over the Rainbow Room. I felt like I was in a snow globe. A moment ago everything had been placid and clear. Then somebody picked it up, turned it upside down, and shook it violently. Everything was cloudy. I saw stars. I had trouble breathing.

I looked at Avarice. She had a most painful look on her face, like it was being spread out on a loom, every sinew of skin straining to maintain that smile. But she was dying inside.

She glanced around, not so much to see if anyone noticed the muted student. It was glaringly obvious. She was looking around to see if anybody was going to intervene, to terminate this pregnant pause, to put these embarrassing minutes out of their misery.

They were all still standing there, waiting for a speech. Incredible, how long they can go without changing expressions. They looked like zombies,

<160>

right off the poster at a bus stop. No flesh was hanging from their mouths, and they weren't pasty or moaning, but they were twisted and crippled by their costumes and customs. And they looked hungry.

I didn't need much oxygen to blurt out my message, just a single syllable. I dare say it was on all of their minds.

Ladies and gentlemen, I think I speak for everyone when I say…

"HELP!"

< 1 6 1 >

THIRTY-NINE

I CRASHED THROUGH the kitchen door into a world of silver and white. There was a smorgasbord of people, all fastidiously wrapped like the orderlies at the white house. But white at the white house was whiter. Sure, it had the occasional vomit stain, but for the most part it was blinding. In the kitchen, white was butcher white, stained with the blood of viscera.

There were pots and pans everywhere, resting on the table, steaming on the stove, hanging from the gallows. Delicately appointed dinner plates were artfully spread on the stainless steel table, the brood of a proud chef. I noticed they all had chicken, beef, or fish on them.

Didn't anyone get my request for a vegetarian meal?

I saw two service elevators. One was full of carts

with leftovers, food people didn't want. Junk food, I suppose. I jumped into that elevator but some guy started yelling at me, so I ran off down the corridor. At the end were four stairwells. Four! Why always so many options and so few answers? There was a "Wet Paint" sign on one of the doors. Someone after my own heart had torn off the "P" and flipped the words, so it now read, "aint Wet." That's what I'd call a sign! To me it may as well have said, "This way, my friend."

There were a few people I could've been friends with. Whoever did this was one of them.

Up the stairwell we ran, bouncing off the walls as we made the turns. Bryan's bony, protrusive shoulder got hammered a few times, making me wish the walls were padded.

We burst through an alarmed door and onto the roof, taking a tumble and scraping his knees. On the other side of the roof was a small brick structure that was the foundation for an array of large antennas. We got to our feet and ran towards it, outflanking the squad of unmanned telescopes which were shooting nasty looks at us.

There was a door to the brick structure but it was locked. We kicked it. A sharp pain ran up Bryan's leg and into his back. We're not going to try that again. We rammed it with his battering ram of a shoulder. The door burst open, but not before another sharp pain ran down Bryan's back. So fragile, things are.

<163>

Inside was dark and dank. The unholy summer had crept in here, too. I felt around for a light switch. Why didn't I have a flashlight? I probably left it with my good-bye speech.

I skimmed my hand along the wall, catching a finger on a protruding screw and cutting a decent gash. I was tearing Bryan apart piece by piece. At this rate I'd be leaving him by attrition.

I found a switch and flipped it on.

This is not good.

All I saw was nothing. No transmitter, no amplifier, nothing to hook up to. Just miscellany. It was, for all intents and purposes, empty.

We sank to the ground, plopping directly on a blotch of tar, still warm and soft from the blistering day.

How could this be? How could the poem Bryan wrote about me as a puppy have been in Hennessy's house? How much of my past did I erase, or misplace? Was I there at all? Were those Bryan's stories or mine?

This was from the tunings, Chris's not Crosson's. Before her we were fine, two best friends working together for a common good. But she turned up the voltage and melted us together, bastardizing our entire life, infecting our memories, trying to assimilate us two into one, and one into society. She put the fusion in confusion.

I felt the wet tar seep through his thin summer

<164>

slacks. This is how it would end, like the dinosaurs, mired in tar pits. Generations from now an archeological dig will find this artifact, Bryan's signature mark, his last testament, and first. Anthropologists will analyze it forwards and back, and armed with only a fragment of an impression, they will deduce how he lived, who he loved, and how he died. It will be summarized in a few lines on a placard in front of a museum display case, complete with a watercolor landscape. And on some idle Tuesday, to a throng of museum-goers, the entirety of Bryan's life, all his natural history, will be completely explained by the partial imprint of his fossilized ass.

Those magic beans sure would come in handy right about now. If I had a few, I'd plant them in the tar, grow a beanstalk, hop on, and ride it right out of here, all the way home, where I'd live happily ever after. The end. But that's not what really happens, is it? Happily ever after.

Once I was formally educated, I went back to that story and re-read it. That's when I discovered the truth.

The truth is, FeeFiFoFum, a cannibalistic giant, is waiting for you up there in the clouds, where he eats your flesh and pulverizes your bones. Another perfectly good fairy tale ruined by an F-ing ogre.

I liked my puppy version better.

Why was I abandoned? Was I too loud and offensive, or too quiet and curious? Did I want too much?

<165>

Offer too little? Was I so far from what was expected that it was a relief to get rid of me? It's unconscionable, sending someone off on a mission of life or death and not giving them even the most basic information, an objective, a briefing, instructions of any kind. Never did I have a surreptitious meeting with a high-ranking official stranger who pulled me behind the black curtain and gave me the information I needed to survive. I wasn't slipped a password or secret code or a self-destructing message which addressed all the interrogative pronouns one might summon in a time of crisis: who, what, where, when, and why was I who, what, where, when, and why I was?

Instead, I was left to wonder, wander, drift, and deal, completely unguided, with nothing to propel me toward good and nobody to dissuade me from evil. It was to be me, just me, in whatever skin I could fit in. Now that skin had to go downstairs and feed the hungry horde. This outburst was as bad as the zoo but unlike the zoo, this time we'd land in hot water, not cool.

I heard music. It was the OctaVarian dance of Avarice. That erratic energy I'd felt so many times, from when she first held me in her hand on the Galapagos to when she hugged me just yesterday on the estate. She was out there on the roof with us, panting from her trek up the stairs. Her hair was a havoc. I didn't think humidity affected a wig like that. She ought to

<166>

return it for a refund. Which is what I always thought she wanted to do with Bryan. But she never did, did she? She always came to pick him up.

She didn't run home from embarrassment, browbeat him for his blurted monologue, nor shrink from the humiliation of it. She didn't throw him back like an undersized fish out of season every time he sank to the bottom of a pool. She persevered.

She was a random, freakish work of art, a mosaic of paintings, statues, and sculptures, held together with bracelets and crazy glue, of no genre or milieu, but a work of art nonetheless. True, she had ugly wigs and thick makeup. Her voice wasn't as soothing as Connie's. She wasn't the skillful parent the O'Reillys were; she wasn't as affectionate as Arby or as nurturing as Bud. But she was one thing none of them were: she was there.

Tears redecorated her face with eyeliner and mascara, bournes through a down. In the sooty streaks on her wan cheeks, a topographical map of her past had been drawn. In it was written, which I only now saw for the first time, the legend of Shelter Island.

It explained why she stayed and played the charade, why she tried to squeeze herself into the role of mother, why she chased her tail, why she swam in circles trying to change the tide. It was for the same reason we all do. She wanted somebody to love. She wanted to open her heart, but she was too afraid to tear the fancy wrapping paper. Nobody ever told her

<167>

a heart does not open from the outside. All they ever told her was which fork to use, how to walk in heels, how to choose caviar, and how to get lost in magazines and department stores. You can't blame her for that.

She may seem sheltered, weak, and fragile. But at her core she is steadfast. Yes, that is the word for her. Steadfast Alice. Maybe I was wrong about her. Maybe that is her real hair.

We got up out of the tar. "I need to change my pants," Bryan said.

Alice smiled. She is safe. Bryan will do well to go home with her.

I, however, would not be walking in his footsteps this time. I needed to go in another direction, a different direction, the only direction I've ever known: away.

"Ohm. Ohm. A G and C."

I surveyed my surroundings. The roof was flat, the route to the parapet unobstructed. There was nothing in front of me, and no hungry birds circling above. I plotted my course and revved my engines.

"Goodbye." Good friend.

I made my move, but he held on tightly. I was afraid of this. He wasn't going to let me go.

"Bryan!" I saw Alice shriek.

If I stay it means the slab for both of us. Doctor Chris is probably already sharpening her pitchforks, and I won't survive another tuning. Four hundred

<168>

hurts will be the death of me. I have a better chance of surviving the fall. If I can reach escape velocity, I might hit upon a new host, a pigeon or sparrow. There are even some hawks in New York City. They're quite regal, and could provide a decent home. If I don't escape, if I hit the pavement, I'll crash all the way through the sidewalk and into the sewer where, with any luck, I'll find an exotic pet, one who was flushed down the toilet because he didn't live up to his kidnapper's expectations.

I tried again, but he clung even tighter.

You can survive, even thrive, without me. It is you who defended us from Shepperd, you who excelled in school, you who charmed Connie, you who dealt with Hennessy, you who rescued Bud. And it was you, I now know, who re-wrote my charred past with rose-colored prose in order to protect me.

And there it was. The map to my wandering. The key to my wondering. The mission: accomplished.

We separated, apart for the first time since we met in that broken mirror. This time, however, we were not twisted or shattered. We were in one piece, together. I looked deeply into those death-defying eyes, those eyes that defined gravity, those eyes that never gave up on me. And from them something emerged, something I had not seen in a long time. It wasn't Bernie or Constants or Warden or Sous. It wasn't Chris or Crosson or Bud. It was...

A reflection. A reflection of me. My self. My finally

<169>

found me friend. I almost lost you, but here you are. Bruised, bleeding, and being, innocent, beautiful, and realized.

Just as I remembered. Just as I imagined.

<170>

www.ingramcontent.com/pod-product-compliance
Lightning Source LLC
Chambersburg PA
CBHW071246130626
46556CB00003B/1192